16

JUNIOR CLASSICS

Published by
Rupa Publications India Pvt. Ltd 2016
7/16, Ansari Road, Daryaganj
New Delhi 110002

Sales centres:
Bengaluru Chennai
Hyderabad Jaipur Kathmandu
Kolkata Mumbai Prayagraj

This is a work of fiction. Names, characters, places and incidents are either the product of the author's imagination or are used fictitiously and any resemblance to any actual person, living or dead, events or locales is entirely coincidental.

P-ISBN: 978-81-291-3900-9
E-ISBN: 978-81-291-4323-5

Third impression 2023

10 9 8 7 6 5 4 3

Printed in India

Contents

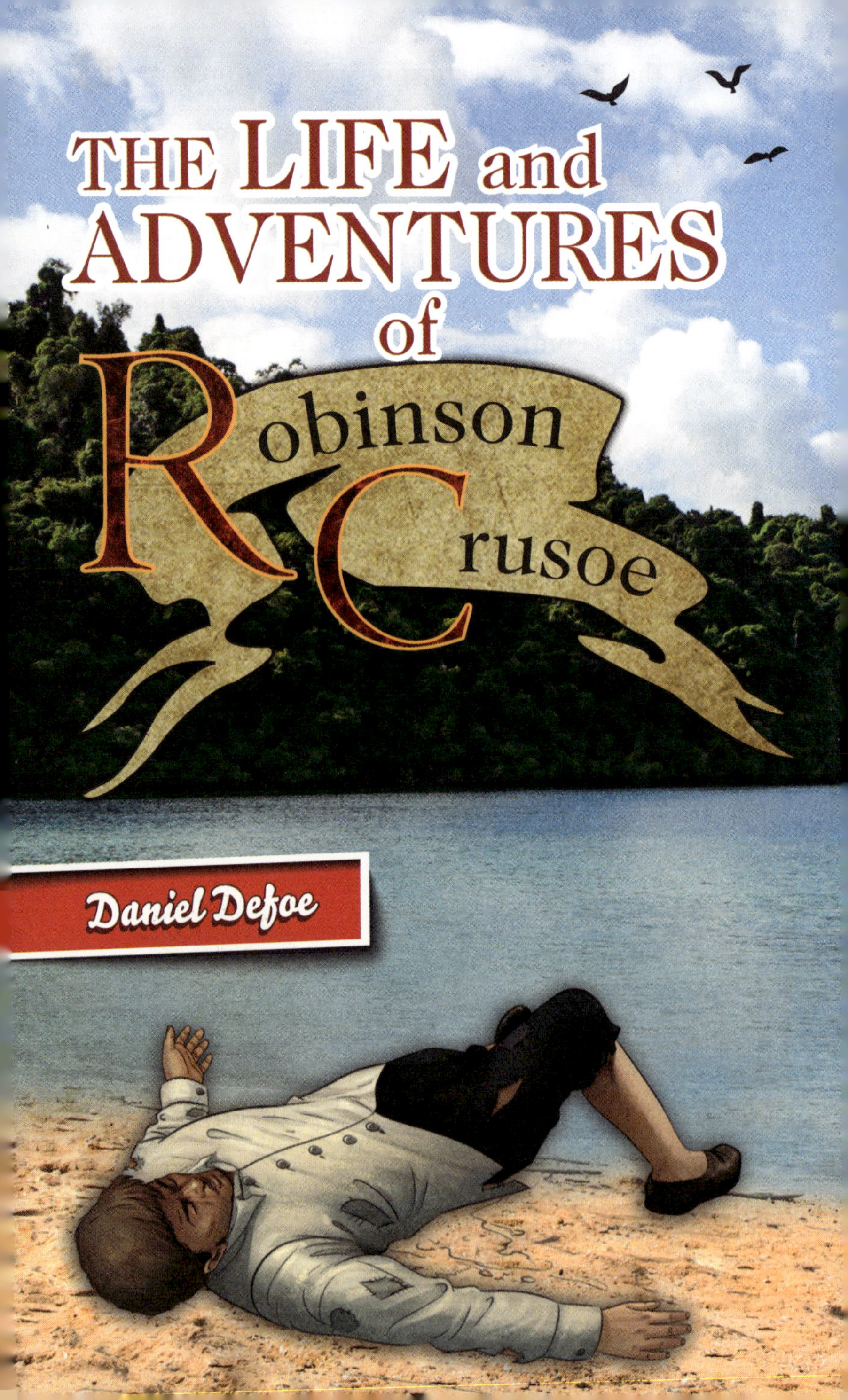
THE LIFE and ADVENTURES of Robinson Crusoe
Daniel Defoe

I was born in the year 1632, in the city of York, and was named Robinson Crusoe. My father wanted me to be a lawyer but I wanted to spend my life at sea. So, on 1 September 1651, I went on board a ship headed for London, against my father's commands and my mother's advice.

Never has any young adventurer's bad luck begun sooner or continued longer than mine. The ship had barely left the coast when the wind began to blow and the sea began to rise. As I had never

been at sea before, I was most sick and terrified. As days went by, I began to see terror and amazement in the faces of the seamen themselves.

While a terrible storm was blowing, I could hear the master praying to the Lord for mercy. I looked out at a dismal sight: waves as high as mountains crashed upon us every three to four minutes. Our men shouted out loud that a ship which rode a mile ahead of us was going to sink. We got into a boat and slowly made our way to the shore. Less than quarter of an hour after we got into the boat, we saw our ship sink.

Had I decided to go back home after this incident, I would have been happy and my father too would have been overjoyed to hear about my survival. But my ill fate pushed me on with an obstinacy that nothing could resist.

After parting with my friends, I travelled to London by land. There I met a captain of a ship and told him that I wanted to see the world. He said that I could travel with him on a voyage to Guinea in Africa at no expense. I agreed.

However, this too turned out to be another unfortunate enterprise. This time our ship was captured by pirates and I was taken as a prisoner to Sallee, a port belonging to the Moors.

One day, my master sent me out for fishing with another Moor and a boy. Hanging onto the opportunity, I grabbed a gun and pushed the Moor into the water. Pointing the gun at his head, I told him to swim towards the shore. Then, I turned towards the boy, Xury, and asked him whether he would accompany me faithfully. Xury agreed.

According to my calculations, we were sailing south towards the Canary Islands. We approached a land where we could see dark, naked people standing on the shore. They beckoned us to stop the boat and offered us some food. We were well supplied with roots and corn, as well as water.

Here, I stepped inside a cabin and sat down to ponder over our situation.

Suddenly, Xury cried out, 'Master, Master, a ship with a sail!'

I jumped out of the cabin and saw that a Portuguese ship was near. I sent a distress signal and fired a gun. On seeing these signals the men, very kindly, sailed towards us. In about three hours' time, I was on board their ship, along with all my goods.

I told the captain that I was an Englishman, who had made an escape out of slavery from the Moors at Sallee. I offered all I had to him, as a return for my release, but he would take nothing.

The captain said, 'I have saved your life in the same way that I would like to be saved myself.'

He promised to deliver me safely to Brazil. Then, he offered to buy my boat for his ship's use. About twenty-two days later, we arrived at the All Saints' Bay.

I lived for almost four years in Brazil, learnt the language and prospered on my plantation. Then, one day, some merchants and planters whom I was familiar with told me that they had a ship which they were planning to take to Guinea. They asked me whether I would accompany them to manage the trading on the coast of Guinea.

As I was born to be my own destroyer, I could not turn down the offer any more than I could restrain my first rambling designs when my father's good counsel was lost upon me. So, I told them I would go with all my heart if they would undertake looking after my plantation in my absence. Soon the ship was ready, the cargo furnished and everything was done as per my agreement with my partners. I went on board in an evil hour on 1 September 1659.

Our ship was about 120 tons heavy. It carried six guns and fourteen men, besides the captain of the ship, his boy and me. We didn't have any large cargo on board. We only carried articles such as beads, bits of glass, shells, knives, scissors and hatchets which were fit for our trade.

We were at seven degrees twenty-two minutes northern latitude, when a violent tornado, or a hurricane, took us by surprise. It had begun from the south-east, moved to the north-west and then settled in the north-east. For twelve days we could do nothing, but let it carry us where luck and the fury of the winds directed.

During this time one of our men died of high fever, while another man and the boy were washed overboard.

On the twelfth day, we concluded that there was no inhabited country for us to have recourse to in the vicinity. So we went in the direction of some of our English islands. But a second storm came upon us soon. This drove us so far out of the way of all human commerce that had we survived, we would be in danger of being destroyed by savages.

While the wind was still blowing very hard one morning, one of our men cried out, 'Land!' Just as we ran out of the cabin to look out, the ship struck upon the sand and stopped. We realized that the ship would break into pieces very soon, and some even said that it had broken already. So we decided to leave the ship and get into a boat.

Though the storm had weakened considerably, the sea waves were still dreadfully high. It soon became clear that the boat could not survive such high waves and we would all drown. After we had rowed about a league and a half, a raging wave came rolling towards the boat and overturned it so suddenly that we were swallowed up by the sea in a moment.

I could swim, yet I could not free myself from the waves to breathe. Eventually, a great wave carried me swiftly towards the shore and left me there. I was now safe and looked up to thank God. I never saw my comrades or any sign of them, except three of their hats, one cap and two shoes.

However, I soon forgot to be thankful when I realized that I was wet, and had neither a change of clothes nor anything to eat or drink. I had no weapon, either to hunt for food or to defend myself with against any other creature. All I had was a knife, a tobacco pipe and a little tobacco in a box. This caused me such agony that I ran about like a madman for a while.

As night-time neared, I wondered what I would do if there were any greedy beasts around. I decided that I would climb a thick bushy tree such as the fir which grew nearby. A little distance away from the shore I found fresh water to drink and I put a little tobacco in my mouth to keep hunger at bay. Next, I cut a short stick for my defence and took up my lodging on the tree. Since I was tired I fell asleep quickly and slept rather comfortably.

When I woke up the next day, I noticed that the ship had been tossed up near a rock and the boat on land. So I made my way to the ship, hoping to find a few things that would be useful for me on a deserted island.

I climbed on board with the help of a rope that was hanging on one side of the ship. The first thing I did was look for dry things and filled my pockets with biscuits.

I decided that it was useless to wish for things which I did not have. Instead, I began putting to use whatever I could find. So, I tied four wooden poles together at both ends to form a raft. Then, I placed two or three short planks on the poles crosswise. I laboured in this way till the raft was able to bear a good amount of weight.

Next, I filled three of the seamen's chest with provisions—bread, rice, Dutch cheese, dried goat's meat, European corn and some liquor. I also managed to secure a couple of pistols, some powder horns, two rusty swords and a carpenter's chest. With great pain and difficulty, I guided my raft to a little cove where I fastened her on a flat piece of land, by sticking two broken oars into the ground on either side of the raft.

My next job was to seek a proper place to live and a safe place to stow my goods. I knew nothing about the land where I was standing on—whether it was an island or a mainland, whether it was inhabited or not and whether there was any danger of wild beasts or not. I noticed a very steep hill about a mile away. I climbed the hill and on reaching the top, my fears were confirmed—I was stuck on an island and there were only two smaller islands nearby.

The island that I was on seemed dry. I noticed a great deal of birds but none that I could recognize or that was fit for eating. On returning to the spot where my raft stood, I began building a fence around myself with the chest and boards that I had brought on shore. I prepared a sort of a hut for that night's stay. However, I had not figured out a food source yet.

I considered returning to the ship and looking for more useful things. So I climbed aboard the ship as before, and prepared a second raft. I unloaded several things—muskets, bullets, clothes, a hammock, a fore-topsail, some bedding. I made a little tent with the sail and some poles, to store my things away from rain and sunshine. I spent about thirteen days going on board the ship and bringing away all that I found useful. I even discovered some money—some European, some Brazilian, some gold and some silver.

I smiled to myself at the sight of this money and said, 'What are you good for? You are not worth taking off the ship. One more knife is worth this entire heap. Go to the bottom of the sea as a useless item whose life is not worth saving.'

However, on second thoughts, I took some with me.

Just as I was thinking of making another raft, the sky became cloudy and the wind began to blow. So I got down from the ship and swam towards my little tent. I sat there with all my wealth about me, feeling secure. The wind blew hard all night and in the morning, when I looked out, no ship was to be seen!

Now, I turned my thoughts towards finding a more secure place and setting up a home there which would protect me from savages and wild beasts. I decided that I needed: first, health and fresh water; second, shelter from the sun; third, safety from greedy creatures; and fourth, a view of the sea so that if God sent any ship I may not lose a chance to be rescued. Thus, I set about in search of a proper place and found a little plain on the side of the hill would be ideal.

Next, I took cables and laid them between two rows of stakes to create a strong fence. This took a lot of time and effort, but I made a fence so strong that neither a man nor an animal could get into it or over it. I made a short ladder so that I could enter this fortress. Once the fence was set up, I brought all my things and stored them in a tent that I had set up in the enclosure.

During this time, I also stepped out once a day with a gun to see if I could kill anything fit for a meal. To my satisfaction, I soon discovered that there were goats on the island. With my first shot I killed a goat, which provided me with meat for quite a while since I ate little and saved my things as much as I could.

I thought a great deal over my condition. Tears would roll down my face as I wondered why God would completely ruin His creatures and leave them so miserable and depressed that one could not be thankful for such a life.

But reason made me think in a different way, 'Well, it is true that your condition is not a very happy one, but recall where the rest of your shipmates are. Didn't eleven men come here in a boat? Why were the rest of them not saved? Is it better to be here or out there in the sea?'

Then it occurred to me how well provided I was.

After I had spent about ten or twelve days on the island, it occurred to me that I would soon lose all notion of time. I didn't have a book, pen or ink to make notes with. So, with a knife I cut capital letters on a large post: I came on shore here on 30 September 1659. This I set up on the shore where I first landed. On this square post I also cut a notch with my knife every day and thus I kept a calendar.

Eventually, I found that I had brought several more things out of the ship, such as pens, ink, paper, charts, instruments and three Bibles. And then I began to keep a daily journal till I ran out of ink and was forced to quit writing.

While I was rummaging through my things, I found a bag which had been filled with corn for feeding the poultry. The corn had been eaten by the rats and all that remained were husks and dust. I shook the husks out and decided to keep the bag for another purpose.

About a month later, I saw a few stems of green shooting out of the ground but thought that it was a plant that I had never seen before. As more time went by, I was astonished to see about ten or twelve corn ears come out, which were perfect green English barley. Near these I saw some other stalks as well, which later proved to be stems of rice. This touched my heart and brought tears to my eyes.

With great care, I saved the corn ears and decided to sow them again, hoping to have a sufficient quantity for myself. But it was not until the fourth year that I gathered enough to allow myself to eat this corn. Even then I had to use it sparingly. I preserved more than twenty or thirty stems of rice with the same care to make food.

I had been on this island for more than ten months when I lost all hope of ever being saved from my condition. I firmly believed that no human had ever set foot here. Here is an excerpt from my journal.

Sept. 30—*I have now come to the unhappy anniversary of my landing. I have cast up the notches on my post and found that I have been on shore three hundred and sixty-five days. On this day I observed a solemn fast, admitted my sins to God, acknowledged His righteous judgements on me and prayed to Him to have mercy on me.*

As the months passed, I realized that the seasons of the year could be divided, not into summer and winter, as in Europe, but into the rainy and dry seasons. According to my observation, the second half of February, the whole of March and the first half of April were rainy. The remaining half of April, the whole of May, June and July and half of August were dry. The remaining half of August, the whole of September and half of October were rainy again. The remaining half of October, the whole of November, December and January and half of February were dry again.

I had a good mind to see the whole island and so, one day, I travelled to the other side. I came within view of the sea and I could clearly see land not less than fifteen or twenty leagues away. I concluded that this must be a part of America. I pondered that had this land been a Spanish coast I would certainly have seen some vessels pass one way or the other. Since that was not the case, this land must be the savage coast between the Spanish country and Brazil. It was perhaps inhabited by the worst savages who are cannibals or man-eaters. I thanked God that I had not landed there.

With these thoughts in my head, I leisurely explored the island. Here, I caught a parrot that I brought home to keep as a pet and teach it to speak. After many months I was able to teach him to call me by my name.

I had no shortage of food available, especially of goats, pigeons and turtles. On this journey, I also found a young goat. I decided to take this kid home and to tame goats. I thought that this exercise would prove to be useful some day if I ran out of bullets to shoot with.

The third year began, and I was seldom idle. I divided my time amongst my daily duties: first, reading the scriptures; second, looking for food which took me more than three hours every morning; and third, the cutting, preserving and cooking from my daily catch.

When four years passed by, I observed my anniversary with the same devotion to the Word of God. I looked upon the world as a remote thing I had nothing to do with. I had enough to eat and supply my needs. If I killed more than I could eat, the vermin would consume it. If I grew more corn than I could eat, it would rot. The most miserly person in the world would have been cured of desire to store had he been in my situation.

However, my clothes had begun to decay. Though I was alone on the island, I could not walk around naked because the heat caused blisters on my skin. I had saved the skins of all the creatures that I killed and hung them up in the sun. With these I made a cap which kept my head dry when it rained, as well as a waistcoat and breeches that protected me from the heat. After a great deal of trial and error, I was also able to make an umbrella which was very helpful both in the rain and the heat.

Now I will relate to you a new scene in my life. One day, when I was going towards my boat at about noon, I was surprised to see a man's naked footprint on the shore. I listened and looked about but could neither hear nor see anything. I went up and down the shore but I found no other impression except for that one. Terrified, I came home.

I could not sleep that night. Sometimes I believed it must be the devil since my mind thought, how should any other thing in human shape come there? Where was the vessel that brought them? Where were the marks of the other footsteps? But to think that Satan would take human shape and leave his footprint behind for no reason seemed funny. The Devil would not leave a mark in a place where there was little chance of my seeing it.

After some thinking I concluded that the footprint must belong to a more dangerous creature—the savages on the opposite mainland who had wandered out in the canoes but had left again not eager to stay on this desolate island.

These thoughts took up many hours, days, even weeks and months. Then, it occurred to me one day that this may be my own footprint. This thought cheered me up a little.

I had completed twenty-three years of my stay on the island and, except for the fear of the savages, was very content with the life I led.

When I stepped out one early morning in December, I was surprised to see a light from a fire on the shore, about two miles away on the island. I observed that there were at least nine naked savages sitting around a small fire, perhaps to dress some of their cruel diet of human flesh. Eventually, they left and it was more than fifteen months before any of them came there again. I was pained by the thought that they would discover me.

It was in the middle of May, on the sixteenth (according to my wooden calendar), I think, that I was surprised by the noise of a gun fired at sea. In great haste I got to the top of the hill and I heard a second shot. I thought that this must be a ship in distress and though I could not help them,

perhaps, they might help me. So I piled up some dry wood and set it on fire on top of the hill.

The fire burned all night and as soon as it was day, I saw something at a great distance which I concluded was a ship. I ran towards it and, to my great sorrow, saw a shipwreck. I don't know whether any men on the ship were saved or not but, some days later, I saw a corpse near the shore.

Days passed and one morning, I was surprised to see five canoes on the shore of the island. I observed, from my hiding place, that there were no less than thirty people dancing around the fire. Next, I saw two miserable men dragged from the boats and brought out for the kill. One of them, seeing a chance for escape, started to run away extremely fast directly towards me. Only three savages ran after him but he managed to outrun his pursuers and I noticed that he would easily get away.

As they neared a creek, only two of the savages were able to swim and follow the fleeing man. I intervened by knocking one of the savages down and shooting another with my gun. Then, I called the poor fleeing savage to come to me. He was

trembling and kneeled down in front of me. When he spoke to me I could not understand his words, but they were pleasant to hear since they were the first sound of a man's voice that I had heard in over twenty-five years. He made a motion to me to lend him my sword and with it he cut off the head of the savage whom I had knocked down. When he had done this, he returned in triumph and laid down the sword and the savage's head at my feet. I took this man to a cave for shelter and gave him food to eat along with some water. Then using signs I suggested that he lie down and sleep.

He was a handsome fellow with straight, strong limbs and he must have been about twenty-six years old. His hair was long and black, his eyes were sparkling and sharp and his skin was dark. When he woke up, he made signs to let me know that he would serve me so long as he lived. I told that I would name him Friday, which was the day I saved his life. I taught him to say 'master', 'yes' and 'no'. Then, I gave Friday a sword and a gun and we went off to the place where the savages had been. We found that the enemies had left but the place was covered with human bones, the ground dyed with blood and pieces of flesh left here and there. I made Friday gather all the skulls, bones and flesh, and burn them all to ashes.

When we returned to my home I gave Friday some clothes to wear which at first he wore awkwardly but soon eased into. I was delighted with my new companion and made it my business to teach him everything that would make him useful; especially to make him speak to me and understand me.

Friday had been with me for three years, and I was spending my twenty-seventh year on the island, when I decided to attempt an escape from my captivity. I worked with Friday to make a canoe which would help us undertake the voyage.

One morning, while I was stocking the canoe with some provisions, I sent Friday to the shore to find a turtle.

Friday returned, crying out loud, 'O Master! O Master!'

'What's the matter, Friday?' I asked.

'Over there,' he said, looking very scared, 'one, two, three canoes!'

I tried to calm him and then loaded four muskets and two pistols with bullets. I went up to the side of the hill and saw that there were twenty-one savages, three prisoners and three canoes on the island.

Friday and I shot down and killed sixteen of them, while four of them escaped and one was wounded. I released the victim and asked him which country he was from. He replied that he was from Spain. Friday took a closer look at one of the victims in the boat and began singing and jumping about. When I could make him speak to me, Friday told me that the victim was his father.

My island was now inhabited with people and I felt like a king with subjects. All of them owed their lives to me and were ready to lay it down for me.

I was fast asleep one morning, when my man Friday came running to me and called aloud, 'Master, Master, they have come!'

I climbed on top of the hill to get a good view and realized that an English ship was approaching. I wondered what business an English ship could have in that part of the world and decided that it was best to be on my guard.

When the men reached the shore I noticed that three of them were unarmed and tied. The cruel seamen left the prisoners and scattered about the island, looking at the country. I marched up to the prisoners to learn about their situation.

I said to them in English, 'Gentlemen, do not be surprised to see me. You seem to be in distress. Tell me about your situation and I might prove to be a friend.'

One of them replied seriously, 'Sir, I was the commander of that ship. My men have mutinied and made me a prisoner. They have set me with these two other men—one, my mate and the other, a passenger—here in this lonely place where we thought we would die.'

I promised to rescue the prisoners on two conditions: that the three men would be governed by my orders on this island and would take me back to

England on their ship. Once I was assured of their consent I handed over three muskets to them. Then, together we devised a strategy and were able to make the mutineers surrender.

The rescued captain and I went on board the ship and prepared to sail immediately. Thus, I left the island after living there for twenty-eight years, two months and nineteen days. I took with me the goatskin cap that I had made, my umbrella and my parrot. After a long voyage I arrived in England on 11 June 1687.

On arrival, I learnt that my father, mother and most of my family had died. Only two sisters and two children belonging to one of my brothers were still alive. On enquiry, I learnt that my plantation in Brazil and its production had been improved. I was now master of more than 5,000 pounds sterling, and had an estate in Brazil which brought me more than 1,000 pounds every year.

I married and became a father to two sons and a daughter. I also adopted my nephews. When my wife died, I embarked on a voyage to my island. I saw that it was now inhabited by the Spaniards and the island had been improved.

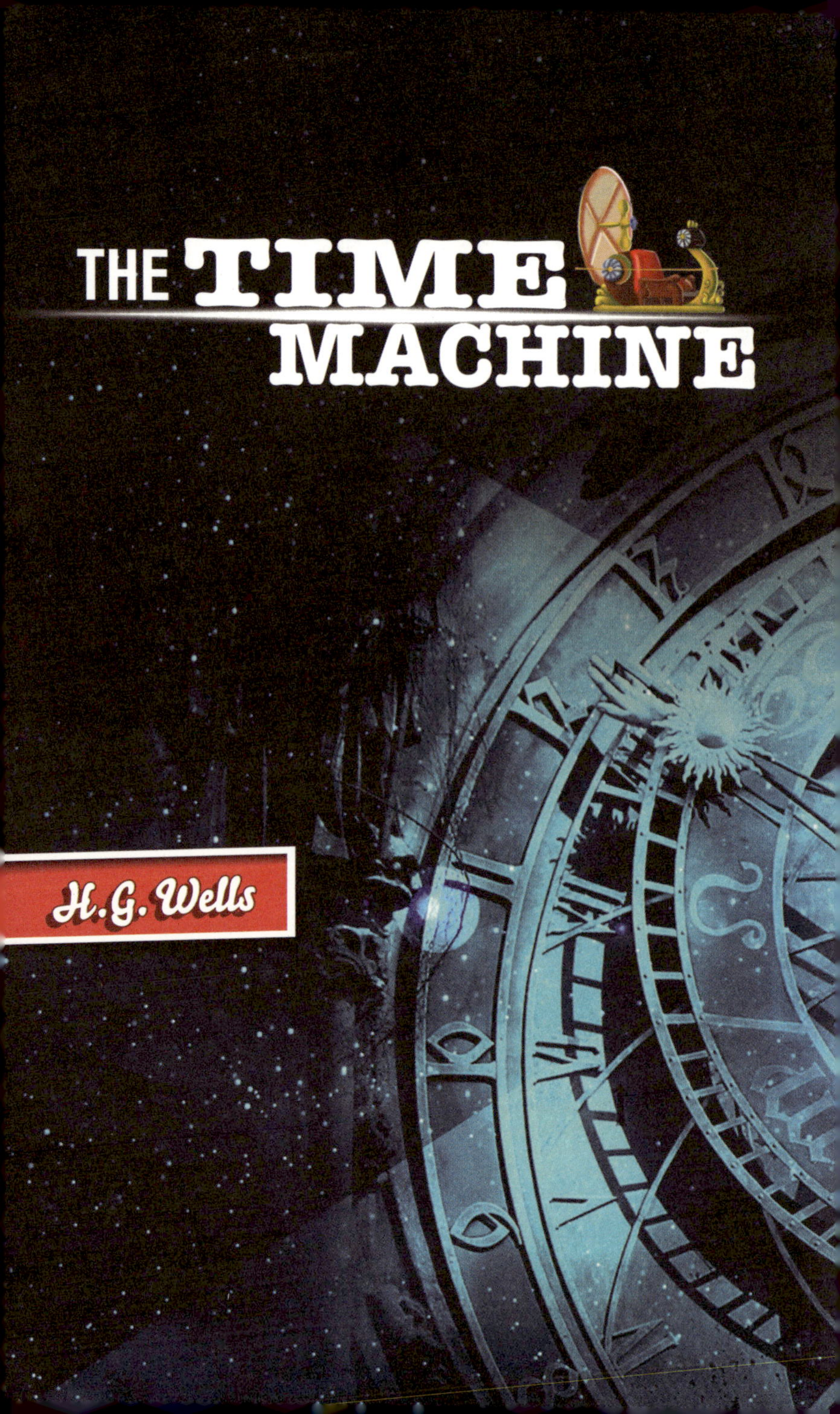
THE TIME MACHINE
H.G. Wells

Our host, we shall refer to him as the Time Traveller, was an great scientist and one evening, after dinner, he was sharing his knowledge with us. His grey eyes shone and twinkled, and his usually pale face was shining and animated.

Apart from the Time Traveller, I was in the company of a doctor, a psychologist, the provincial mayor and a young editor.

'In order to follow my point,' said the Time Traveller, 'you have to be prepared to revise your understanding of the universally accepted laws of geometry. I do not ask you to accept anything without reasonable ground for it.'

'That's fine,' said the psychologist.

'Any real body must exist in four dimensions,' the Time Traveller went on. 'It must have length, breadth, height and *duration*. There are really four dimensions; three of which we call the three planes of space, and the fourth one is time. There is no difference between time and any of the three dimensions of space.'

'But,' objected the doctor, 'if time really is the fourth dimension of space, then why is it regarded as something different? And why can't we move in time as we move about in the other dimensions of space?'

The Time Traveller smiled.

'Are you sure we can move freely in space?' he asked. 'I admit that we can freely move backwards and forwards but, how about up and down? Gravitation limits us there.'

He explained that balloons and rockets are only devices to counter the force of gravity. Hence, he concluded, it is neither correct to claim free movement in space, nor is it correct to assume that we can't move in time.

The Time Traveller told us that he had been unwilling to discuss the topic until he had experimentally verified this capability. Now he wanted to show us his invention and walked towards his laboratory. The guests were sure that he would return with some sleight-of-hand tricks.

He returned with an instrument, the size of a small clock. It had a metallic frame and was delicately made using ivory and some transparent crystalline substances.

'This little apparatus,' said the Time Traveller, 'is only a model of a machine that allows time travel. It took me two years to make it.'

He explained to us how the apparatus worked. Pointing at two levers, he said that pressing one would send the machine gliding into the future, while pressing the other would send it into the past. The apparatus was also provided with a saddle for a Time Traveller.

He urged the psychologist to turn the lever. I am sure that no trickery was involved. A breath of wind blew and the lamp flame jumped. The little machine suddenly swung around, grew indistinct, like a ghost, and then—vanished!

Everyone was silent for a minute.

Then the Time Traveller laughed and asked, 'Would you like to see the Time Machine itself?'

He took the lamp in his hand and led us to his laboratory. There we saw a larger edition of the little mechanism that had vanished before our eyes. It was made, in part, of ivory, nickel and rock crystal.

It was almost complete except for the crystalline bars that lay unfinished beside some sheets of drawings.

'On that,' said the Time Traveller, 'I plan to explore time.'

All of us were a little confused and not sure how to take it.

***

The next Thursday, I went to Richmond again to meet the Time Traveller. I found four or five men already assembled in his drawing room. Besides the doctor and the psychologist, there were three other men in the room that day—an editor of a well-known newspaper, a journalist and another quiet, shy man whom I didn't know.

It was half-past seven when the doctor suggested that we have dinner. He said that the Time Traveller had left a note, asking everyone to move for dinner in case he wasn't back till seven.

There was some speculation about the host's absence at the dinner table. I jokingly mentioned that he might be time travelling. Just as the psychologist offered to inform the new guests, the door opened slowly and without a sound. We saw the Time Traveller standing before us.

'Good heavens! What's the matter?' cried the doctor.

The Time Traveller appeared to be in complete disarray. His coat was dusty and dirty and covered with green down the sleeves. His hair was dishevelled and appeared greyer than it used to be. His face was pale and his chin had a half-healed brown cut on it. For a moment he hesitated at the doorway, as if dazzled by the light. Then

he limped in to the room. We stared at him in silence, expecting him to speak.

Without uttering a word he drank a glass of champagne. His eyes grew brighter and a faint colour returned to his cheeks.

'I'm all right,' he said at last. 'I'm going to wash and dress and then I'll explain things. Save me some of that mutton. I'm starving for a bit of meat.'

As he walked towards the staircase I saw that his feet had nothing on them but a pair of tattered blood-stained socks. When he returned, the Time Traveller looked normal except for his tired appearance.

'I want something to eat,' he said. 'I won't say a word until I get some peptone into my arteries.'

At last, after he had eaten his fill, the Time Traveller led us to the smoking room. He agreed to tell us his story.

'I was in my laboratory at four o'clock and since then… I've lived eight days…' with that the Time Traveller began his story as I have reproduced it here.

'I had explained the principles of the Time Machine to some of you. I completed the Time Machine this morning and at ten o'clock today, the machine undertook its first journey. I pressed the start lever with one hand and then almost immediately pressed the stop lever with the other. For a brief instant, I felt a nightmarish sensation of falling. Then I looked at the clock. A moment ago, it had stood at a minute past ten; then it was almost half-past three!

'I drew a breath, held the starting lever with both hands and went off with a thud. The laboratory became hazy and dark. Mrs Watchett, the housekeeper, came in and walked towards the garden door. It must have taken her a minute to do so, but to me she seemed to shoot across the room like a rocket. I pressed the lever over to its extreme position. Night came on suddenly and was instantly followed by day. This repeated unendingly. The laboratory grew fainter and fainter and finally disappeared. A buzz-like sound filled my ears and I became confused. The feeling of a helpless headlong motion was quite unpleasant.

'As the speed increased, nights and days chased each other in quick order. Then, days and nights merged into a continuous greyness. The sun looked like a streak of fire across the sky and the moon looked like a faint band of light.

'I was still on the hillside upon which my house stood. I saw generations of trees growing and changing; huge buildings came up and passed off like dreams. I covered a whole year and more in just one minute. I was curious to know what kind of civilizations rushed before my eyes. However, stopping the machine could result in a crash if, in the future, a solid substance occupied the space that the machine and I occupied. As long as I was in motion with such velocity, I was slipping like a vapour and did not bump into a stationary object. But to stop meant to bring atoms of two objects into such an intimate contact that a chemical reaction would result and could cause an explosion. Finally, I pulled the stop lever and the machine went reeling over, tossing me headlong through the air.

'I found myself sitting in a garden, surrounded by rhododendron bushes. A severe hailstorm was beating down and in a minute I was wet to the skin. A very large figure, carved of white marble, resembling a winged sphinx, stood beyond the bushes. The pedestal appeared to be of bronze.

'As the hailstorm lifted, I saw other shapes too—huge buildings with tall columns, along the hillside. A sudden fear seized me. I felt naked in a strange world. I grabbed the Time Machine and turned it over. The possibility of a quick retreat gave me some courage. I was able to look less fearfully at the world of the distant future.

'Then I heard voices approaching me. Some men were running towards me through the bushes. The one who reached first was a small creature—about four feet high—dressed in a purple tunic and a leather belt. He wore sandal-like footwear and his legs were bare to the knees.

'He looked very beautiful and graceful, though frail. I suddenly gained confidence and withdrew my hands from the Time Machine. The man came straight up to me and smiled. The complete absence of fear seemed remarkable.

'Soon, a little group of eight or ten of them had gathered around. They spoke in a strange and

very sweet language. I felt that my voice was too harsh and deep for them. So I avoided speaking to them. They touched my hands and shoulders, wanting to make sure that I was real. I had to warn them to keep their hands away from the Time Machine though. I unfasten and pocketed the two levers for safekeeping.

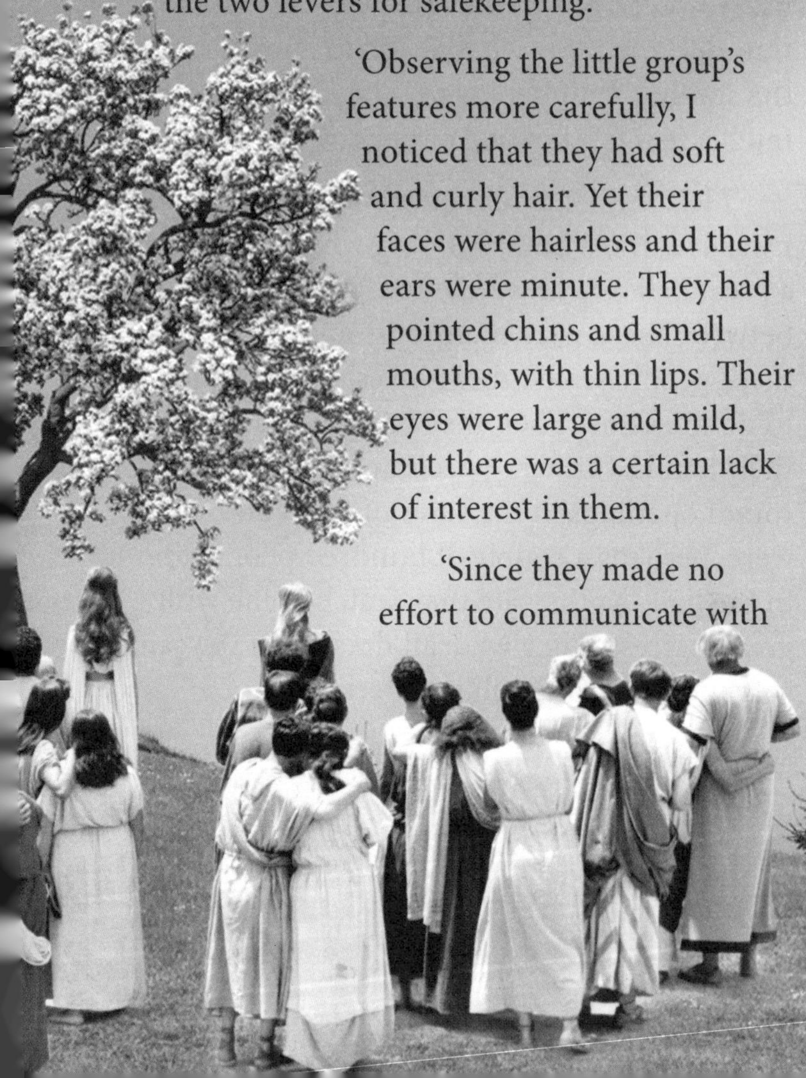

'Observing the little group's features more carefully, I noticed that they had soft and curly hair. Yet their faces were hairless and their ears were minute. They had pointed chins and small mouths, with thin lips. Their eyes were large and mild, but there was a certain lack of interest in them.

'Since they made no effort to communicate with

me, but simply stood about smiling, I began the conversation. First, I pointed towards the Time Machine and myself. Then, in order to express the word time, I pointed at the sun. I had assumed that the people in the year 802000 AD or so would be far more knowledgeable and intelligent than us. However, one of them copied the sound of thunder to ask me whether I had come from the sun in a thunderstorm. They showed the intellectual level of one of our five-year-olds.

'I left the Time Machine and followed them. I was led into a huge building which opened into a great hall. There were numerous tables and between these were many cushions on which these people seated themselves and signalled me to do the same. Then they began to eat fruits with their hands, throwing peels and stalks into the round openings in the sides of the tables. There were, perhaps a couple of hundred people dining in the hall. As they ate they watched me with great interest. They were all dressed in the same soft and yet strong, silky material.

'These people of the remote future were strict vegetarians and only ate fruits. I found out later that most of the animals, such as horses, sheep and dogs, had become extinct.

'Once I had eaten enough, I decided to learn their language. It seemed easy to begin with the names of fruits. I picked up each fruit and made gestures and sounds, asking for its name. Soon I had learnt the names of a few fruits, some pronouns and even the verb 'to eat'. However, this was slow work since their interest in everything was very short-lived.

'As I emerged from the great hall after the meal, the scene outside was lit by the warm glow of the setting sun. I noticed that, over the years, the Thames had perhaps shifted a mile from its position. I walked up a hill to have a better view of the surroundings. I saw ruins of ancient buildings scattered around. Apparently, the single house system for every family had vanished. Here and there among the greenery were palace-like buildings.

'That's when I realized that everyone wore the same costume, had the same soft hairless face and the same round limbs. There seemed to be no difference between the genders and the children seemed to be small versions of their parents.

'While I was thinking on all that I had observed, a pretty little structure caught my attention. It was a well under a cupola. I looked around and saw that there were no large buildings towards the top of the hill. So, I started climbing up to the crest. The sun had already gone below the horizon and the west was a flaming gold, touched by some horizontal bars of purple and crimson. Below was the valley of Thames, in which the river lay like a strip of polished steel. The great palaces dotted the greenery, some in ruins and some still occupied. Here and there rose the sharp vertical lines of some cupola or obelisk. There were no hedges, no signs of private property and no evidence of agriculture. The whole earth had become a garden.

'As the full moon rose from the north-east, the little figures ceased to move about. The night was growing cold and I decided to climb down and find a place to sleep.

'I looked for the building which I had visited earlier that day. My eye caught sight of the figure of a white sphinx but I was shocked to see that the Time Machine was not where I had left it. I started to worry about my future and of being left helpless in this strange new world. I ran around, crazily searching among the bushes. I was sure that no one could have accidently turned on the machine; once the levers had been removed the machine would not start. I cried aloud but no one answered. Not a single creature seemed to stir in that moonlit world.

'I went to the great stone building. The big hall was dark, silent and deserted. I lit a match and went in to the adjoining hall. Here I found a score or so of the little people sleeping.

"Where is my Time Machine?" I shouted, like an angry child.

'Then abruptly I threw the match down and rushed out, knocking down one or two of them on the way out. For a long time, I groped and searched on the moonlit ground. Finally, I lay down and slept near the sphinx.

'When I woke up the next day with a cool head, I decided to be patient and tactful. If it had been taken away I must recover it by tact or if necessary, by force.

'I examined the ground again where the machine had stood. In the daylight I saw a noticeable route, between where the machine had stood and the sphinx's pedestal. I looked at the pedestal and found that it was made of bronze. Knocking on it disclosed that the pedestal was hollow inside. It was now clear that the Time Machine was inside the pedestal. However, I did not know how it got there or how to take it out.

'Two of the little people were walking by and I called them to come towards me. When they came near, I explained to them that I wanted to open the pedestal. The fellows seemed to be shocked and walked off as though I had insulted them. I tried a sweet-looking chap next but received the same result. In my desperation, I caught hold of the man and began dragging him towards the sphinx but seeing the hateful expression on his face I let him go.

'I banged on the bronze panels with my fist and heard a sound, like a chuckle, from inside the pedestal. Then, I took a big pebble and hit the panels with it. A crowd of the little people watched me but nothing came of my efforts.

'After this incident the little people seemed to avoid me for a day or two. I decided to put away my thoughts about my Time Machine, until I had enough knowledge to lead me back to it in a natural way. So I tried to focus on learning the little people's language. Their language was very simple, free of abstract terms. Their sentences were usually simple and of two words.

'My explorations disclosed several round wells, concentrated on the hill slopes. I could not see what lay at the bottom but could hear a certain sound: thud-thud-thud. Another strange aspect was that there were only big palaces for living purposes. There were no workshops, no machinery or appliances. The people seemed to spend all their time in playing gently, bathing in the river, eating fruit and sleeping.

'One morning, while I watched the people swimming in the river, I noticed that one of them was seized by a sudden cramp and was drowning. No one made an attempt to rescue the weak, crying little thing. I jumped into the river and carried her to safety.

'Later that day, when she spotted me she greeted me with delight and gave me with a big garland of flowers. I learnt that her name was Weena and we became good friends. She was exactly like a child and wanted to follow me everywhere. Nevertheless she was, somehow, of great comfort to me.

'It was from Weena that I learnt that fear had not yet left the world. She was fearless during the day but she hated the dark and shadows. I realized that no one could ever be found outdoors or even sleeping alone indoors after dark.

'One night, close to dawn, I noticed movement at the foot of the hill. I think I saw a lonely white, ape-like creature running rather quickly up the hill. Another day, I found a narrow dark gallery. When I entered, I was spellbound. A pair of luminous eyes looked at me out of the darkness. The queer figure had flaxen hair on its head and down its back. I followed the creature until the human spider clambered down a well. I sat looking down the well for a long time, thinking about the new world order. Finally I concluded that humans had not remained one species, but had changed into two distinct animals. This bleached nocturnal thing was also man's heir. This second species had taken to living underground.

'I guessed that the earth must be tunnelled and these tunnels were the habitat of the new race. The presence of airy shafts and wells everywhere showed their extent. I knew that the beautiful race above the ground was called 'Eloi'. 'Morlocks' was the name by which the underground dwellers were known.

'When I asked Weena about these dwellers, she shivered as though the topic was unendurable. When I pressed her with my questions, she burst into tears.

'I began to share the Eloi's disgust of the Morlocks. The pale bodies were just like half-bleached worms preserved in spirit in glass jars. I knew that I had to deal with the Morlocks if I wanted to regain my Time Machine, but I recoiled from the very thought of it.

'Meanwhile, I continued to explore London. While in a region now called Combe Wood, I saw an old, porcelain-green building which appeared larger than any mansion I had come across so far. I went to examine it with little Weena by my side. When I attempted to climb down a well to explore, Weena gave a desperate cry and started pulling me back. I smiled at her but continued to climb down using hooks and handles. As I lowered myself, I heard the thudding sound of machines, loud and oppressive.

'I lit a match and saw three stooping white creatures hastily rushing for cover along a tunnel. The light from the match hurt their eyes. I crawled through the tunnel and reached a large cave-like open space with large machines. There was a white metal table in the centre of the cavern with a meal of fresh meat on it. It was clear that the Morlocks were carnivorous. The match in my hand burned out and I was left with only four matches in my pocket.

'As I stood in the dark, I sensed a strange unpleasant odour and a crowd breathing around me. The Morlocks grabbed me and laughed in strange voices. I freed myself by striking another match and went back into the tunnel. Finally, I made it to the top and fell upon my face in the blinding sunlight. There I saw Weena, waiting for me along with a few other Elois.

'After this incident, Weena and I continued to roam around as I thought over the new world order. Occasionally, Weena darted off to pick flowers which she placed in my pockets.'

The Time Traveller paused, put his hand into his pocket and silently placed two dried up flowers, upon the table. Then he resumed his narrative.

'At around noon one day, we reached the porcelain-green palace again. It was a great deserted ruin. We entered a long gallery and I realized that the place must have once been a museum. The gallery housed the paleontology section and held huge skeletons. Another gallery was devoted to minerals and other geological specimens. Here I found a sealed box of matches and a jar of camphor. I also picked up an iron lever, to serve as a mace for defence. With these in my possession I felt more confident and secure.

'When we left the green palace the sun was still above the horizon. I decided that we must

cross the woods before nightfall. I wanted to walk as far as possible before building a fire and resting under the protection of its glare. However, it was night time before we reached the woods.

'The Morlocks were beginning to move about behind the bushes. I calculated that if Weena and I could cut across the mile-long forest and reach the bare hillside, we would have a safer resting place. I dropped the firewood and dry grass I had collected on the way, and set fire to it. This was to frighten the Morlocks as well as to cover our path.

'While walking through the woods, at first, I could only hear the crackling twigs under my feet and the faint rustle of the breeze. Then I heard a distinct steps about us. It became evident that the Morlocks were closing in upon us. It was time to light a match. For this I had to put Weena, whom I had been carrying on my shoulders, down on the ground.

'I could feel soft little hands moving over my coat and back. I searched blindly in my pockets for a match. A struggle began. Finally, the flaring match revealed the white backs of Morlocks in flight. When I looked for Weena, I found her lying quite motionless, clutching my feet. She was barely breathing.

'I decided to build a fire and settled in at that very spot. Very soon a smoky fire was lit and I turned my attention towards Weena. However, despite my best efforts I could not revive her.

'I was weary from the exertion and nodded off. When I woke up the fire had gone out. I was being pulled down by my hair, neck and arms. I felt as if I was in a monstrous spider's web and could feel little teeth nipping at my neck.

'As I rolled over, my hand fell on the iron lever. It gave me strength. I struggled up and struck the Morlock's faces with the lever. I could hear the cracking of flesh and bones under my blows.

'Suddenly, the Morlock army started running away. Sparks flew overhead. The fire that I had started outside the forest had spread and was consuming the forest.

'I frantically looked for Weena but there was no sign of her. She was gone. With the fire raging there was no time left. I ran ahead of the fire and soon reached a small open space. The fire had caused so much confusion amongst the Morlocks that some even ran straight into it. I could not find Weena anywhere and, at last, sat down on the top of the hillock, exhausted and sad.

'The next day, I searched for Weena again. I was sure that the Morlocks had left her poor little body in the forest since they could not have carried her away in such a fuss. I was relieved to think that she had escaped the awful fate to which she seemed destined.

'I walked slowly, feeling wretched about Weena's death, till I reached the place where the Time Machine was kept hidden.

'At about eight or nine in the morning, I reached the ruins of the hill overlooking the white sphinx. The Eloi were moving about in their bright robes.

'I was sad to think how brief the glory of human intellect had been. This is what the human race had declined and evolved into. This is what had happened to the human race through its hankering after comfort, ease and permanency. There is no intelligence where there is neither change nor need of change. Such is the law of nature, I pondered. The Morlocks overcoming the taboos of cannibalism and preying on the Elois was also a part of this degeneration.

'Exhausted, I fell asleep and woke up just a little before sunset. With the iron lever in hand, I headed towards the white sphinx. To my surprise,

I found the bronze panels of the pedestal lying wide open. There was a small room inside and the Time Machine stood in a far corner of the room. Was this the Morlock's surrender after the great devastation by fire the previous night? Or was this a devilish trap?

'When I reached the Time Machine, I was surprised to see that it had been carefully oiled and cleaned. They seemed much superior to the Eloi.

'As I stood there, examining the Time Machine, suddenly the bronze panels banged shut

and I was trapped. I could hear the Morlocks's gleeful chuckles all around. I was not upset. I only had to fix the levers and depart like a ghost.

'The little brutes were very close and one even touched me. I made a sweeping blow in the dark at them with the levers in one hand and searched about for the machine's saddle with the other. This struggle was a closer shave than the one in the forest.

'At last, I managed to fit the levers and pull them. The clinging hands slipped off from me and the darkness cleared. Once again, I was into the grey haze and rush of travelling through time. I had left behind the year 802701 AD along with its inhabitants.

'I clung to the machine as it moved and vibrated. When I looked at the dials, I was amazed to find that the hands were spinning around the dial into futurity. I had pulled the levers to make them go forward.

'As I moved ahead in time, I noticed peculiar changes. Though I was travelling with incalculable speed, the alternations of night and day grew slower. The passage of the sun across the sky also slowed down, to a point where it seemed to stretch for centuries. At last a steady twilight sat upon over the earth—there were no more nights and days. At last, just before I stopped, the earth had come to rest with one face to the sun. Here, I saw monstrous crab-like creatures and huge butterflies. Eventually, as I continued travelling, all traces of animals and birds disappeared. Darkness spread through the day and surrounded the earth. I felt nauseous and faint. A terrible dread of lying helpless on that remote and awful beach made me clamber back on my saddle.

'Thus, I returned. As I travelled back through time everything that had happened on my way out was reversed. The hands spun backwards on the dials. At last, the old walls of the laboratory came round me.

'The timepiece on the table showed that it was eight in the evening and I heard voices coming from the dining room,' he concluded.

The whole story was still beyond the guests' imagination and belief.

'What a pity it is that you're not a story writer,' said the editor.

The doctor said, after some hesitation, that the Time Traveller was suffering from overwork. The Time Traveller responded with a loud laughter. Soon the dinner was over and as his guests departed, he stood in the open doorway calling out 'Good night' to them.

I was disturbed by the fantastic story and the honest and sober way in which it was narrated to us. The next day I returned to the Time Traveller's house.

'I'm very busy with that thing in there,' he said, holding a small camera under one arm and a knapsack under the other, pointing towards the machine in the laboratory.

He walked down the corridor and banged the laboratory door shut. I followed and on opening the door, I saw a ghostly indistinctive figure sitting on a whirling mass of black and brass. Suddenly, the Time Machine and the Time Traveller were gone.

I waited for the man to return with his second adventure story, the specimens and photographs. However, I am beginning to fear that I must wait a lifetime. It has been three years since the Time Traveller set out on his second journey.

KIDNAPPED

Robert Louis Stevenson

I will begin the story of my adventures with a certain early morning in the month of June in 1751. As I walked away from my father's house and down the road, I found Mr Campbell, the minister of Essendean, waiting for me by the garden gate.

'Davie,' he said, as Mr Campbell walked beside me, 'when your mother passed away and your father was on his deathbed, he put me in charge of a letter, which he told me was your inheritance.'

The letter that he handed over to me was addressed in these words: 'To Ebenezer Balfour, Esquire, of Shaws.' Mr Campbell asked me to be at my best behaviour at the house of Shaws and then, before parting, he gave me three gifts—a shilling, a Bible and a recipe to make curative water from lilies.

My heart was beating fast at this great chance which lay before a poor country boy, only seventeen. I was happy to get away out of that quiet countryside and go to a great busy house to live among rich and respected gentlefolk of my own name and blood. So I set ahead on my journey towards Cramond, near Edinburgh.

The next day at noon, I reached the top of a hill from where I could see the city of Edinburgh with its castle and its ships. On reaching Cramond, I asked for directions to the house of

Shaws. My queries were met with strange looks. I began to think there was something strange about the Shaws. It was nearing sunset when I approached a fat woman for directions, and she pointed at a great building which looked like a ruin. No road led up to it, no smoke arose from any of its chimneys and there was no sign of a garden.

The woman said in a loud, angry voice, 'That is the house of Shaws! Blood built it and blood shall bring it down.'

Cautiously, I walked up to the door and knocked. When I received no response I began to kick the door and shout out aloud for Mr Balfour. A man wearing a nightcap and holding a gun appeared at the first-floor window.

When I told him that I, David Balfour, had brought a letter of introduction from my father, the man guessed that my father must have passed away and he allowed me to enter the house.

A mean-looking, narrow-shouldered, stooping man opened the door and told me to go into the kitchen. The table in the kitchen was laid for supper with a bowl of porridge and a mug of beer.

The man introduced himself as my uncle, Ebenezer Balfour. He must have been between fifty and seventy years old. He offered me his porridge for dinner and said that he would drink the beer. I wondered why my uncle never looked at me straight in the eyes.

After dinner, Uncle Ebenezer led me through a dark entry to show me my room. He told me that he didn't like lamps or candles in the house because he feared fires. When I entered the room, I heard him turn the key and lock the room from outside. The room was cold and the bed damp, so I laid down on the floor and fell asleep.

When I woke up, I noticed that the room was large and furnished with embroidered furniture. Ten or twenty years ago, it must have been a pleasant room to lie down in. However, lack of use had done much harm. I had to knock and shout to get my uncle to release me.

The breakfast at the table was the same as the previous night's meal. This time, my uncle offered me some beer too.

I spent the day going through a great number of English and Latin books which I found in the room next to the kitchen. While doing so, I discovered a book that had a note written on an inside page in my father's handwriting. It read: *A gift to my brother Ebenezer on his fifth birthday.* I was confused by this note. Until then, I had presumed that my father was my uncle's younger brother, but the writing was neat like that of a man's.

When I asked Uncle Ebenezer whether he was my father's younger brother or whether they were twins, my uncle grew angry, jumped upon his stool and caught hold of my jacket. At the same time he declared his love for my dead father which puzzled me. On the one hand, I began to think that my uncle was perhaps mad and might even be dangerous. On the other hand, I remembered a folktale of a wicked relative who tried to keep a poor boy away from his rightful heir. I

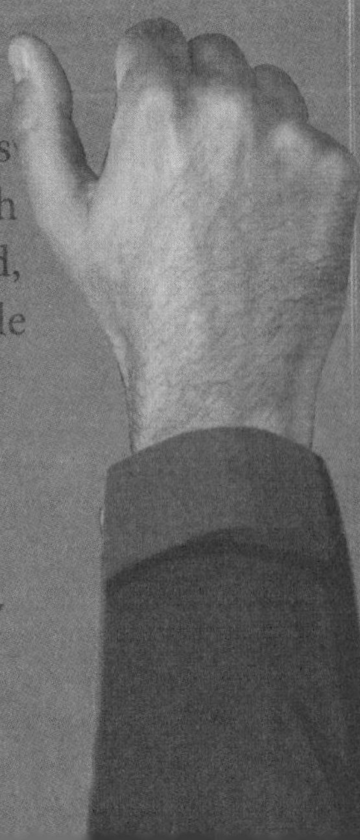

began to wonder if my uncle had some reason to be afraid of me.

Next, Uncle Ebenezer gave me thirty-seven golden guineas and told me that the money was a part of the promise he had made to my father. I said that I would like to prove my gratitude to him. He replied that he was growing old and would like me to help him around the house. So he told me to fetch a chest from the tower at the far end of the house. I asked him if I could have a light to show me the way. He repeated that no lights were to be used in his house but that the stairs were good.

The house of Shaws was five-floor high. I kept close to the wall and inched my way up the stairway, my heart beating fast. When a lightning flashed I faced a scary view. I seemed to have been climbing up an open scaffold, and my next step would have led to my fall. I became very angry when I realized that my uncle had sent me, perhaps, to die. I groped my way down again and caught my uncle by surprise. Stunned to see me alive, Uncle Ebenezer fell

to the floor like a dead man. I sprinkled some water on his face and asked him for an explanation regarding his behaviour. My uncle said he wasn't feeling well and begged me to let him go to bed. So I locked him in his room and went back to the kitchen to sleep.

The next morning, I woke up and thought about all that had happened the previous night. There was no doubt about my uncle's enmity, but I was confident that I was clever enough to deal with him. I released him from his room, and could see that he was trying to prepare a lie for an account of the previous night's events. As we sat at the kitchen table, a cabin boy brought a letter for my uncle. The letter was from the captain of a ship named *Covenant* and the captain had requested my uncle to come to Queen's Ferry immediately. Uncle Ebenezer explained to me that he had some business with the captain. He suggested that I accompany him to the ship, so that after dealing with the captain we could go meet a lawyer, Mr Rankeillor, to clear any doubts that I had. I was excited to get a good view of the sea and the ships and so agreed to go to the ferry.

On the way to the Queen's Ferry, Ransome, the cabin boy, spoke to me and boasted about the many wild and bad things he had done. He also talked about the ill-treatment he had to face at the hands of his masters which made me feel sorry for him.

Eventually, we reached the Hawes Inn and met Captain Hoseason. While Uncle Ebenezer and the Captain were busy in a discussion in a room, I decided to wander around. I ran into the innkeeper who told me that I looked like my father, Alexander Balfour, and then warned me about my uncle's nature. He disclosed that according to a rumour my uncle had killed my father.

Once the meeting was over, the captain invited me to step aboard his ship. The captain assured me that the ship would drop me near Rankeillor's house. So I agreed and was thrilled to see the ship. Soon I found myself on the ship's deck.

'But where is my uncle?' I asked suddenly.

I ran to look over the ship's side and saw my uncle sitting in another boat that was heading for the town.

'Help, help!' I screamed. 'Murder!'

Strong hands pulled me back from the ship's side. I felt as if a thunderbolt had struck me and I fell down unconscious.

When I regained consciousness, I was in great pain and realized that my hands and legs were tied. I guessed that the ship was now sailing on the sea. As I lay in misery, Mr Riach, a short man with green eyes, about thirty years old came to offer me some brandy and water. He argued with the captain that I was unwell and should be moved to a berth in another part of the ship.

So I was moved and found a berth where I stayed for many days, getting back my health.

Here, I came to know my companions, the sailors. I came to a conclusion that no class of human beings is all bad, and these shipmates were no exception to the rule. They showed signs of kindness and honesty.

The ship was headed for the Carolinas and in those days white men were sold into slavery on the plantations. That was the destiny to which my wicked uncle had condemned me.

Ransome came in at times to share with me the bad treatment he had to bear at the hands of Mr Shuan, another seaman. One night, we all heard that Mr Shuan had killed Ransome.

Before we could come to terms with this news, Captain Hoseason walked right up to me and said to me, in a surprisingly kind tone, 'My man, we want you to serve in the round-house.' I was to take Ransome's position.

The round-house was six feet above the deck. My job was to serve meals. It was an easy one and I was even glad that the work kept me from brooding over my fate.

On the tenth afternoon of the journey, when the *Covenant* was sailing south, thick, wet, white fog set in. That night the ship hit a boat, killing everyone on it except for one man, who was brought in to the round-house. The man was short, but strong and agile. He looked calm despite what had happened. He was dressed in expensive clothes: a hat with feathers, a red waistcoat, breeches of black plush and a blue coat with silver buttons. At the round-house, he took off his coat and laid two silver-mounted pistols on the table.

Speaking in a Scottish accent, he introduced himself as a Jacobite, a supporter of King James II and a Catholic. He offered Captain Hoseason sixty guineas to take him to his country—Linnhe Loch. To this the captain agreed.

Later, when I was left alone with the stranger he asked me to fetch some liquor for him. I went to the storage and there, I overheard the captain and Mr Riach making a plan to kill the stranger and take his bag of money. The duo asked me to fetch the pistols from the round-house, telling me that they would share the stranger's gold with me. Though my conscience denied me permission to be a part of the murder, I told them that I would do as they wished. When I reached the round-house, I disclosed the captain's evil plans to the stranger. The stranger introduced himself to me as Alan Breck Stewart, and together we planned a defence.

Alan put me in charge of a cutlass, a powder horn, a bag of bullets and all the pistols. I stood by the window of the round-house to keep an eye out for the captain's men while Alan stood guard at the door.

First, the captain appeared outside the door. When Alan scared him, the captain ran away. A little while later, Mr Shuan approached the round-house and I told Alan that he was Ransome's murderer. Alan pierced Mr Shuan with a sword and killed him.

Suddenly, I noticed five men moving in our direction. Without delay, I shot at them with the gun. The shot killed one and the other four fled in fear. As we waited, a swarm of men came rushing through the door and another attempted to enter through the skylight. I shot my pistol again, killed another man and wounded one more. Alan dealt with the rest of them and drove them out on the deck.

Now, the round-house was in mess; three men lay dead inside and another lay in agony across the threshold. Alan and I remained unhurt.

Through the remaining night, Alan and I took turns guarding the round-house. In the morning, both of us took our drinks and sat down to talk. Alan praised my fighting skills and handed me a silver button from his coat, to express his gratitude and friendship. During our conversation, I was shocked to hear Alan's story—he had been a soldier in the British army, but had joined hands with the Jacobites at the Battle of Prestonpans.

Every year, Alan visited Scotland to select men for recruitment in the French army. He also collected rent from the tenants of the Highlands, who willingly paid the sum for their exiled chief, Ardshiel.

Alan told me that Ardshiel's half-brother, James Stewart, managed the finances for Ardshiel.

When I shared my own story with Alan, and mentioned Mr Campbell, the minister of Esendean, Alan became furious. He said that he hated all the Campbells because a man named Colin Campbell, also known as the Red Fox, was a representative of King George and had kicked the Stewarts out of their homes by using tricks and cheating.

***

As night came, the weather grew rough. Captain Hoseason came to the round-house, asking Alan to help pilot the ship since he was short of crew. Together, the captain and Alan, managed to dodge the ship away from the reefs. However, just when we thought we were safe, a high wave tossed the ship and threw me into the sea. I did not know how to swim but grabbed a wooden pole and held on to it for a long while. Kicking and splashing, I reached a sandy bay surrounded by low hills. There was no sign of a man or an animal. I was afraid to be in such a lonely place.

At daybreak, I climbed a bumpy hill for a better view. I could see no sign of the *Covenant*

and imagined that it must have sunk. I looked at the houses across the island on the mainland with desperation. A flicker of hope arose within me when I spotted a boat coming towards me. But the boat passed by without listening to my cry of help. Fortunately, the boat returned the next morning. One of the people on board used signs to explain to me that when the tide was out the water was shallow enough for me to walk in. So I dashed through the water and landed across with a shout.

At the Isle of Mull, which I had now reached, I came across an old man who sat outside his house. With the little English that he could speak, he explained to me that my shipmates had reached safely ashore. Alan had even left a message for me. He wanted me to follow him to his country, near Torosay. After a filling meal and a relaxed nap at the old man's house I began my journey towards Torosay.

On the way, a blind man offered to guide me to Torosay, despite his handicap. As we walked on, he started talking to me and asking sharp questions. I threatened to shoot him with my pistol if he did not mind his ways. At once the man became very polite until, he turned at the end of a hill and disappeared completely.

Tired and weary after the walk, I reached an inn at Torosay and became friendly with the innkeeper. I asked the innkeeper whether Alan had stayed there or had left any message for me. But the innkeeper did not recognize Alan's silver button. As we talked, I told him about the blind person I had come across. The innkeeper said that I was lucky to get away as that man was a highway robber and has even been accused of murder. At last, he showed me where I could lay down and there I rested for the night.

The next day, I took a ferry from Torosay to Kinlochaline on the mainland. Though the ferry

was crowded, the good nature of the people and their Gaelic boat-songs lifted my spirits.

At Kinlochaline I got an opportunity to speak with Neil Roy Macrob, the captain of our ferry boat. Neil advised me to stay in a public inn at Kinlochaline and resume my journey the next morning. He also told me to avoid the Campbells and the Red Soldiers.

The inn at Kinlochaline was the poorest place that could be and was full of smoke and pests. The next day, when I was on my way, I met a friendly man, Mr Henderland, who invited me to spend the night at his place. I did so willingly. Before we went to bed he offered me six pence to help me on my way. Since he was so eager I accepted it though I left him poorer than myself.

***

The next day, Mr Henderland introduced me to a man who had a boat and was heading out

to Alan's country of Appin. With the help of the boatman I reached the woods of Lettermore in Appin. From here I planned to go to Aucharn, where James Stewart lived.

While I was sitting in the woods, I noticed four travellers riding towards me. The first was a great, red-headed gentleman; the second seemed to be a lawyer; the third was a servant; and the fourth looked like a sheriff's officer. I stopped the troop and asked one of them the way to Aucharn. I didn't realize that the man I was talking to was none other than Colin Campbell, whom they called the Red Fox. Suddenly, while I was busy in a conversation with him, I heard a gun fire and Colin Campbell cried out loud, 'Oh, I am dead!' He sighed and passed away.

While everyone crowded around the dead man, I began to run up the hill, shouting, 'The murderer! I see him.'

The murderer had begun to run. I noticed that he was a big man in a black coat with metal buttons. Meanwhile, Campbell's men, who assumed that I was an accomplice sent to distract them, began chasing me.

Scared, I looked around and, suddenly, heard a voice from behind the trees call me. Astonished, I found Alan standing inside the shelter of the trees. He prompted me to follow him and we ran towards Balachulish. My sides ached and as soon as we were safe, I collapsed on the ground.

When I regained consciousness, I questioned Alan about the killing. I had seen a murder being committed; a jovial gentleman struck out of life in a moment. Alan swore that he had nothing to do with the killing. However, he said that we must leave the country because the whole of Appin would be thoroughly searched. I agreed to go with him.

As night fell we made our way through the woods and reached James's house. James greeted Alan in Gaelic and invited him inside the house.

'This has been a tragic accident,' he told Alan, referring to the murder. 'It will bring trouble.'

Alan remarked that Colin Campbell was dead and James should be thankful for that. James disclosed that he feared for his family. He warned us that when Campbell's men came looking for us, he would share our description since he didn't want to get arrested. Alan agreed but I objected since I had nothing to do with the murder. I told them that a warrant should be put out for the

murderer and we should free ourselves of the false accusation. This shocked Alan and James who had no intention of getting the real killer caught. So, reluctantly, I agreed to go along with Alan. James provided us with some clothes, food and ammunition to aid our journey.

Alan and I made our escape in the darkness of the night. By daybreak, we had reached a valley with mountains on one side and a river on the other. To avoid being caught by the Red Soldiers, Alan decided that we would hide behind the rocks in the river. He jumped on to a rock and I followed.

The rocks had turned slippery due to the constant flow of water. Fear gripped my heart and a drink helped some blood rush back to my brain. Alan set off running for his life and I walked unsteadily behind him.

At nightfall, we washed ourselves in a stream, drank some water and filled our stomachs with oatmeal. Then we set forth in the dark again towards the mountain.

Early in the day, we reached our destination—the Heugh of Corrynakiegh, a cleft in the head of a great mountain with a stream running through it and a shallow cave in a rock. For the next five days we camped in the cave, making porridge, grilling trout and sleeping on beds made of heather bushes.

On the fifth night, Alan decided to send a message to James about his safety. He went to the house of John Breck Maccoll, a friend of the Stewarts, and left a blackened cross with a silver button at his window. Sure enough, Breck visited us the next day at the cave and carried back a letter for James on behalf of Alan. He returned three days later with a packet of money from James's wife. Breck also brought us the news that the red coats were roaming the country and that James and some of his servants had been arrested.

Once again Alan and I continued on our tiring journey. Half the time we had to crawl on our bellies or run on our knees. At the end of it my body felt

bruised and sore. Both Alan and I were weary, so we decided that one would rest while the other stood guard. When it was my turn to guard, I fell asleep. I snapped out of my sleep when I heard the sound of hoofs and saw the red soldiers at a distance. I cautioned Alan and we hid behind a thick heather bush. When the soldiers settled themselves for the night, we quietly moved on our journey.

The next day, as we were coming down the mountain we met four rough-looking men who turned out to be the followers of Alan's friend—Cluny Macpherson. The men took Alan's message to Cluny and in a short while returned with Cluny's invitation for us.

At last, we reached a strange house which was known as Cluny's Den. A tree, which grew out from the hillside, served as the central beam of the roof. The walls were covered with moss and the whole house was in the shape of an egg.

After a delightful lunch, when Cluny set the table for a game of cards, I excused myself in order to rest. On the morning of the third day, I woke up well-rested although a little weak. I noticed that Cluny and Alan had put the cards aside and Alan had an odd look on his face. He told me that he had lost all his money as well as that which he had borrowed from me, to Cluny in card games. I was angry but when it was time for us to leave, Cluny returned our money.

As Alan and I continued on our journey, neither spoke to the other for a long time. I was angry and proud, while Alan was angry and ashamed.

At last, when he could bear it no longer, Alan came close to me and said, 'David, this is no way for friends to treat a small accident. I have said that I am sorry.'

I refused to have a conversation and silence reigned on. We travelled for three nights on strange mountains and wild rivers. The continuous wind and rain made me quite unwell. When my condition worsened and I felt that I would die, Alan lent me his arm. He took me to the nearest house so that I could nurse my wounds. His kindness made my hatred fade away.

Alan knocked at the door of the first house that we came to. By good luck it turned out to be a house of Duncan Dhu Maclaren—a friend of the Stewarts. A doctor was called for to attend to me immediately. Here I rested for a month. During the day, Alan hid in a hole in a little wood and at night he would come to visit me and would not leave my side.

One day, Robin Oig, the son of the notorious Rob Roy, paid a visit at Duncan's house. He enquired a great deal about my family. He wanted to know whether I was related to another Balfour, a gentleman, who once helped Oig's brother. As I knew little of my own ancestry and could not help, Oig turned his back on me in disgust.

On his way out, Oig met Alan at the door. Rob's and Alan's clans were on sour terms with each other and the two got ready for a fight. However, Duncan Dhu interrupted the two, and instead, suggested that the two compete at playing the bagpipe. When Robin took up the bagpipe, he played a fine piece of music from Alan's country. Hearing this, Alan's anger died away. Thus, the quarrel was put to an end.

After I had regained my health and was strong again, Alan and I started again our journey.

On a pleasant day, in August, we said goodbye to Duncan and his family. We decided to head south, cross the Forth River and head to Edinburgh. But we had no boat. So, I pretended to be sick and Alan pretended that we were gentry. He won the sympathy of a young woman at an inn who borrowed a boat and rowed us across the river. We were at a loss of words and could not thank her enough for such kindness.

When we reached Queen's Ferry, I walked up and down the streets looking for Mr Rankeillor. It was by chance that, after wandering for a while, I walked right up to Mr Rankeillor's house in the afternoon. I introduced myself as David Balfour and he invited me into his house to hear my tale of adventure.

Mr Rankeillor told me that Uncle Ebenezer was my father's younger brother and a very handsome man when he was young. Then the lawyer shared the family history with me. My father and my uncle had run away from home to join the rebels in 1715. When they returned, they both fell in love with the same woman. The lady, however, chose my father. My uncle became very angry and took to drinking. At last the two brothers came to an agreement. My father left the estate for his brother and lived with my mother in poverty.

The lawyer assured me that I was the heir to the estate and it did not matter what my father had agreed to. We could not go to court to claim my inheritance, as it would waste a great deal of time and money apart from raising a public scandal. So we made another plan and Alan joined us to execute it.

Alan walked up to Uncle Ebenezer's house and knocked on the door. When my uncle answered the door, Alan told him that he had found me after a shipwreck and held on to me. He demanded money from my uncle in lieu of my release. My uncle didn't want to pay and so Alan threatened to kill me. My uncle did not want me to be killed so he bargained over the price and in the process admitted that he had originally sent me away to be a slave.

At this point, Rankeillor and I revealed ourselves from our hiding place. Fearing a lawsuit, my uncle agreed to draw up an agreement with the lawyer. According to the agreement, I would receive two-thirds of the Shaws's annual income, while uncle would keep a third of the estate.

The next morning it was time to bid Alan goodbye. I planned to send some money to Alan so that he could find a safe passage to France. Alan arranged for a lawyer from whom he could receive the money I sent for him. After these arrangements were made, I shook Alan's hands and parted from him with much grief in my heart.

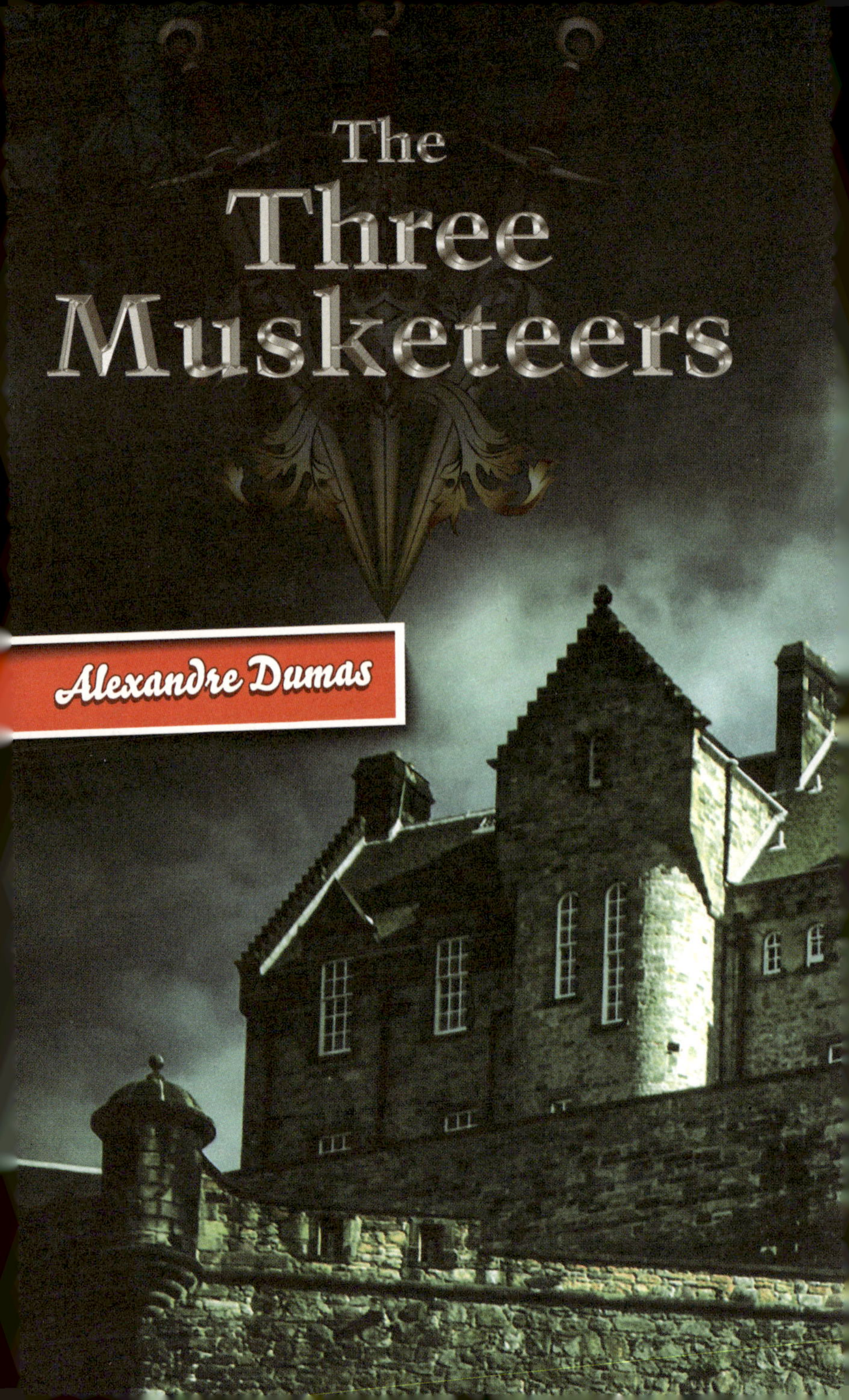
The Three Musketeers
Alexandre Dumas

On the first Monday in April, 1625, the market town of Meung appeared to be in the middle of a revolution. In those times, panic was common. The French nobles fought with each other; the king fought with the cardinal and Spain carried on wars against the French king.

That Monday, when the people rushed towards the noise they saw a young man, dressed in shabby clothes, wearing a cap with a feather and hanging a long sword by his side. The young man rode an equally strange-looking pony. This pony had been a gift to the young d'Artagnan of Gascony, who now rode it, given to him by his father. The elder Monsieur d'Artagnan had also given his son fifteen crowns and a letter of introduction to M. de Treville, captain of the musketeers and the third most important person in the kingdom.

The passers-by, who had looked at d'Artagnan and seen his eyes gleam with ferocity, tried to hold back their laughter. d'Artagnan noticed a gentleman, about forty-five years old, standing with a group of people at an inn and laughing at his appearance. Angry, the young Gascon drew his sword and charged towards the gentleman. Seeing this, the two spectators and the gentleman attacked d'Artagnan with sticks and shovels. The shower of blows left young d'Artagnan unconscious on the ground, covered with blood.

People from all sides had come flocking to the scene of action. Afraid of the consequences, the innkeeper, with the help of his servants, carried the wounded man into the kitchen.

While d'Artagnan was unconscious, the host stole the letter addressed to M. de Treville and showed it to the Gascon's adversary. When d'Artagnan recovered consciousness, the innkeeper insisted that d'Artagnan should leave as soon as possible. He said that the police would deal with the young man quite severely for having fought with a great lord.

As d'Artagnan stepped downstairs to depart, he saw that his adversary was in conversation with a young woman in a carriage who was being referred to as Milady. However, both the gentleman and the lady took off when they saw that d'Artagnan was getting ready to cause another disturbance.

When the time came to pay the innkeeper, d'Artagnan put his hands in his pocket and realized that the letter addressed to M. de Treville had disappeared.

'My letter of recommendation!' cried the Gascon who had depended on entering the king's service based on the letter. 'It contained my fortune!'

First the innkeeper pretended to order an earnest search for the letter. Then he said that he suspected d'Artagnan's adversary of the theft. The Gascon decided to complain of the theft to M. de Treville who would then complain to the king. He paid the innkeeper and, since he needed the money, went to sell his horse for three crowns, just outside Paris.

Thus, d'Artagnan entered Paris on foot, carrying his jacket under his arm, and rented an apartment that was available for a small amount of money. Next, he had a new blade fit to his sword and mended his clothes. Then he retired to bed. The next morning he headed towards M. de Treville's headquarters.

M. de Treville was also from Gascony and had been M. d'Artagnan's neighbour. M. de Treville had arrived in Paris without a penny in his pocket but had become the king's favourite in no time on account of his bravery, intelligence and audacity. King Louis XIII had made M. de Treville the captain of the most loyal guards to the king, the musketeers.

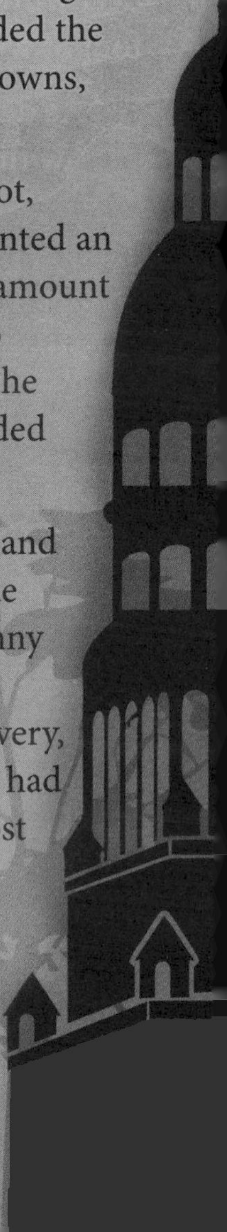

Seeing that Louis XIII had surrounded himself with this formidable body, the cardinal, a powerful rival to the king, too desired to have a company of

guards. So, the cardinal established his own musketeers, and the two rivals tried to find for themselves the most talented swordsmen from all over the world. It was common for Cardinal Richelieu and King Louis XIII to meet for a game of chess every evening and dispute over the merits of their servants.

When d'Artagnan reached the captain's headquarters, he introduced himself to a servant and requested him for a moment's audience with M. de Treville. While he waited, the Gascon observed a group of musketeers there.

D'Artagnan was showed into an office. Here M. de Trivelle made the young man wait while the captain finished his business with the others.

M. de Trivelle called out loudly, 'Athos! Porthos! Aramis!'

Two of the musketeers, Porthos and Aramis, entered and closed the door behind them. M. de Treville paced three or four times in silence before he turned towards them angrily.

'Do you know what the King said to me?' cried M. de Treville. 'He told me that from now on he should recruit his musketeers from among the Cardinal's guards.'

He went on to say that the cardinal had informed the king the previous evening, with an air of condolence, that those 'daredevil' musketeers had created a riot in a cabaret and that a party of his guards had been forced to arrest the rioters.

Porthos explained that though they were six musketeers against the six guards, the musketeers were not captured by fair means. Before they could draw their swords, two of their men were killed and Athos was badly wounded. However, Aramis assured that he had killed one of the guards. Hearing this M. de Treville softened and admitted that perhaps the cardinal had exaggerated. At this moment, a noble but pale face appeared in the room.

'Athos!' cried the two musketeers.

Athos, though wounded, was in full uniform and in a calm voice said that he was there to receive his orders. M. de Treville was moved to affection on seeing this proof of courage. Just then Athos collapsed on the floor.

'A surgeon!' cried M. de Treville. 'A surgeon! The King's! The best! Or my brave Athos will die!'

A surgeon appeared and Athos was carried to another chamber. Once Athos had recovered, M. de Treville returned to his waiting visitor.

Responding to M. de Treville's enquiry, d'Artagnan introduced himself and gave an account of all that had happened on his way to Paris. Then the young man disclosed his desire to be a musketeer. M. de Treville warned him to stay away from the adversary whom d'Artagnan had described.

Suddenly, M. de Treville was astonished to see his student, who had looked outside the window, spring up and turn red in the face.

'Ah, the traitor!' cried out d'Artagnan as he rushed out of the room, leaving M. de Treville looking confused.

D'Artagnan had spotted the man from Meung and chased after him. On his way he bumped into the injured Athos at the stairs. Although the Gascon asked forgiveness and explained that he was in a hurry, Athos was furious and did not accept the apology. He told d'Artagnan to meet him at noon so that the musketeer could cut off the young Gascon's ears. In his haste, d'Artagnan agreed.

As he continued running, the Gascon bumped in to Pathos next and was challenged to yet another duel, set for one o'clock that afternoon.

Soon d'Artagnan lost sight of the man he was chasing but spotted Aramis instead. He interfered in a conversation that the musketeer was having and annoyed the man. Aramis pointed out d'Artagnan's rudeness and the two set a fight for two o'clock that day.

Athos and d'Artagnan arrived at the place agreed upon for a duel. d'Artagnan felt sorry about the pain he had caused Athos by bumping into the musketeer's injured shoulder. He offered his mother's balm to Athos. The musketeer was touched by d'Artagnan's kind gesture but the duel could not be forgotten.

Just then, Porthos and Aramis arrived at the scene to be Athos' witnesses to the duel. Athos explained to d'Artagnan that the three were always found together and were known as the 'Three Inseparables'.

After the introductions were over, Athos and d'Artagnan drew their swords. But barely had the two rapiers clashed, when a company of the cardinal's guards, commanded by M. de Jussac, arrived. The guards wanted to arrest the musketeers for holding a fight which was against the law. The three

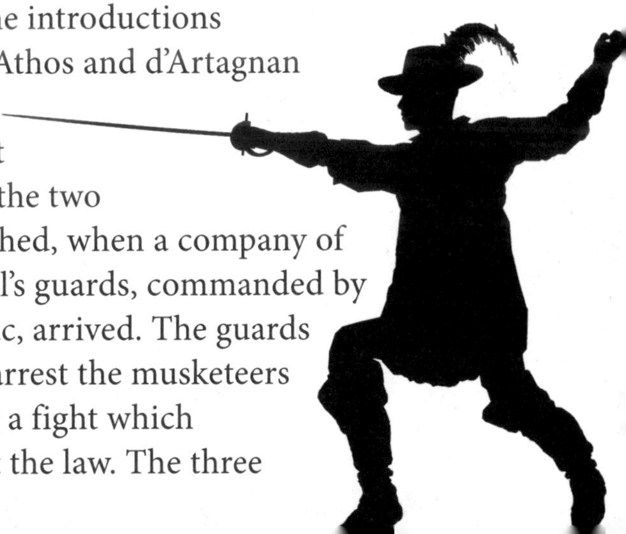

musketeers put up a fight and d'Artagnan joined them.

The Gascon fought like an angry tiger and Jussac required all his skill to protect himself against an adversary who, active and energetic, attacked him on all sides at once. Jussac began to lose his patience and began to make mistakes while d'Artagnan, though lacking in practice, doubled his agility. d'Artagnan stabbed Jussac with his sword and then recued Athos from his assailant.

Together Athos, Porthos, Aramis and d'Artagnan defeated the cardinal's guards. Then, intoxicated with joy, the three musketeers and d'Artagnan marched triumphantly towards M. de Treville's headquarters.

M. de Treville congratulated all four and then quickly headed over to meet the king. As the captain had feared, the news of the brawl had already been brought to the king by the cardinal, who had also made a complaint against the musketeers. M. de Treville assured the king that the musketeers were as meek as lambs but were forced to defend themselves against the cardinal's guards. He requested the king to think over why the five guards had come armed to a lonely place, if it was not to seek trouble.

'Three of the King's musketeers—one of whom was wounded—and a young man not only maintained their ground against five of the most terrible of the cardinal's guards, but fought four of them to death,' gloated M. de Treville.

'Why, this is victory!' cried the king, pleased to hear about his musketeers' courage. 'Did you say, four men, one of them wounded, and a youth?'

At the king's request, M. de Treville gave the details of the battle and impressed the king with d'Artagnan's bravery. The king summoned all four men so he could thank them for their devotion. Pleased with d'Artagnan, the king awarded him forty gold coins.

'Oh, sire!' cried the four companions, with one voice, 'we would allow ourselves to be cut to pieces in your Majesty's service.'

D'Artaganan consulted his new friends on the best use of the gifts given to him. Athos advised him to first employ a servant and Porthos found one, named Planchet, for him.

After this incident, the four friends began to lead a happy life. Every morning, they first reported for duty to M. de Treville. Even though d'Artagnan was not a musketeer, he did the duty of one with remarkable punctuality. Soon he became well known at the headquarters of the musketeers. M. de Treville, who had appreciated him and felt a real affection towards him, never ceased recommending the young Gascon to the king.

The three musketeers too became very attached to their young comrade. The Inseparables were constantly seeking each other three or four times a day, whether for dueling, business or pleasure.

One fine morning, the king commanded M. de Chevalier Dessessart to admit d'Artagnan as a cadet in his company of Guards, since there was no space to admit another musketeer. Thus, d'Artagnan donned his uniform and began his service. Athos, Porthos and Aramis too kept guard with d'Artagnan when he was on duty.

The good days didn't last long for the three musketeers. They soon ran out of money and had to take a loan from M. de Treville. When the inconvenience became distressful, the four, along with their servants, had to take advantage of the free meals offered to one or the other of them.

One day, d'Artagnan's landlord, M. Bonacieux, approached the young man.

The landlord said that he had a wife, who was a seamstress to the queen.

'Monsieur,' he said, 'my wife was kidnapped yesterday morning, as she was coming out of her workroom.'

M. Bonacieux explained that he suspected his wife's kidnapping had something to do with her knowledge of the queen's affair with the Duke of Buckingham. The queen believed that someone had written to the Duke of Buckingham in her name, inviting him to come to Paris and to draw him into a trap. The landlord was afraid that his wife has been kidnapped to either scare her, in order to obtain her Majesty's secrets, or to use his wife as a spy. He also told d'Artagnan that the man who kidnapped his wife was probably one of the cardinal's men.

'Have you seen him?' asked d'Artagnan.

'Yes, my wife pointed him out to me one day,' replied M. Bonacieux. 'He seems to be a nobleman, with black hair, a dark complexion and a scar on his temple.'

D'Artagnan was surprised; the landlord had just described the man from Meung. M. Bonacieux promised that he would be willing to overlook d'Artagnan's rent in lieu of some help in finding his wife.

When M. Bonacieux had left, d'Artagnan shared the news of the kidnapping with the three musketeers. Suddenly, the door was violently thrown open and M. Bonacieux rushed into the chamber where the meeting was being held.

'Save me, gentlemen!' he cried. 'There are four men who have come to arrest me. Save me!'

The musketeers rose and pulled out their swords but d'Artagnan stopped them and said, 'It is not courage but good judgement that is needed.'

When the four guards appeared at the door, d'Artagnan invited them in. He told the guards that he had no intention of protecting M. Bonacieux against the guards' orders. He explained that he had seen M. Bonacieux for the first time that very day when the landlord had come to demand the rent for his lodging. Then d'Artagnan asked the guards to take the landlord and put him in prison. After the guards left, Athos and Aramis congratulated d'Artagnan for the way he handled the situation but Porthos was confused.

'Attention!' said d'Artagnan, as if he had done nothing but command all his life. 'From this moment, we are at war with the cardinal.'

Soon afterwards, the cardinal's guards set up a trap in Bonacieux's apartment. They arrested everyone who visited the house, and questioned them about Madame Bonacieux and her husband.

Since a separate entrance led to the first floor where d'Artagnan lodged, those who called on him were freed from this detention. From his windows, d'Artagnan watched all the visitors who were caught. Then, he removed a plank from his floor, and overheard all that passed between the inquisitors and the accused.

One evening he heard a woman's voice.

'Gentlemen, I am the mistress of the house! I am Madame Bonacieux. I belong to the queen!' cried the woman.

Then he heard sounds of struggle, and d'Artagnan rushed downstairs and entered Bonacieux's house.

Within ten minutes d'Artagnan threw the unarmed officers out of the house. The young Gascon then turned his attention towards Madame Bonacieux, a charming woman, about twenty-five years old, with dark hair and blue eyes. D'Artagnan informed her that her husband had been arrested and asked her how she had escaped from her abductors.

'I took advantage of a moment when they left me alone,' she explained. 'I hurried home since I thought my husband would be here.'

D'Artagnan took Madame Bonacieux to Athos's house. Not finding the musketeer at home, the young man left the lady there and asked her to lock the door.

Following the lady's instructions, he then headed to the palace to meet Monsieur Laporte, the queen's cloak bearer and Madame Bonacieux's godfather. He informed M. Laporte of all that had happened and gave the man Madame Bonacieux's location. M. Laporte advised d'Artagnan to head off to a friend's house who could state in a court of law that d'Artagnan had been with his friend and not at the palace at about half past nine.

D'Artagnan rushed to M. de Treville's house and turned the hands of the clock in the house to half past nine. When M. de Treville walked in, d'Artagnan told him all that he knew about the queen as well as the cardinal's plan. M. de Treville thanked the young man for the information and told him to always keep in mind his service to the king and the queen. Without being noticed, d'Artagnan set the clock at the right time before leaving.

When d'Artagnan returned home, Planchet informed him that the cardinal's guards had arrested Athos. The musketeer had been at d'Artagnan's lodging and was mistaken for the Gascon. Athos had whispered to Planchet to maintain silence since d'Artagnan needed his freedom at the moment.

D'Artagnan decided to inform M. de Treville's house. On the way to the headquarters, he noticed that Madame Bonacieux was walking with a man disguised as a musketeer. Assuming that the lady must be in trouble, d'Artagnan stopped them and drew out his sword. However, Madame Bonacieux explained that the man was the Duke of Buckingham. When d'Artagnan learnt his mistake, he apologized and took the two safely to the palace and then returned home.

At the Louvre, the Duke of Buckingham met the twenty-six-year-old Queen of France. The duke declared his undying love for the queen. The queen responded by pleading with him to leave Paris since it was not safe for the duke to be there. She then gave him a token to remember her by. The duke promised to return within six months and then, after kissing the queen's hand, left the apartment.

Meanwhile, M. Bonacieux was being interrogated in the Bastille prison. M. Bonacieux admitted that he had requested d'Artagnan's aid to help find his wife. The landlord was then taken to meet Cardinal Richelieu. When the landlord promised to keep an eye on his wife and tell her activities to the cardinal, he was allowed to leave.

Next, the Comte de Rochefort, the man who was suspected of kidnapping M. Bonacieux's wife, entered the cardinal's chamber and informed him about the queen's meeting with the duke. He also told the cardinal that the queen had gifted the duke her diamond studs, which His Majesty had earlier presented to the queen.

On receiving this information, the cardinal sent a letter to a lady, asking her to attend a ball that the duke was likely to be present at and steal two of the diamond studs that he would wear.

Meanwhile, M. de Treville had learnt of Athos' arrest and he went to speak to the king about it. He found that the cardinal was also with the king. M. de Treville informed the king that the cardinal's guards had gone to d'Artagnan's house and arrested Athos, one of his majesty's musketeers, without any cause. When the cardinal questioned M. de Treville about d'Artagnan, he was assured that the Gascon had been with the captain himself at about half past nine, the time in question. On hearing this, the cardinal allowed the king to free Athos. M. de Treville left, happy but fearing the reason behind the cardinal's sudden yielding.

The moment M. de Treville left the two alone, the cardinal turned to the king and informed him of the Duke of Buckingham's secret visit to Paris.

The cardinal hinted that the duke had tried to involve the Queen of France in his political project. The king also began to suspect the queen; he believed that she must have written a letter to the duke. So, His Majesty ordered the chancellor to examine the queen's papers.

After completing his mission, the Chancellor handed over a letter to the king which the queen had written to the King of Spain, asking him to plan an attack against the cardinal. On hearing this, the king was glad that no scandal had been discovered and he told this to the cardinal. The cardinal advised the king to throw a ball in the queen's honour, to make up for the insult that the queen had to bear. He also hinted that the king should ask his wife to wear the diamond studs gifted to her. So, the king fixed a date for the ball.

When Madame Bonacieux arrived at the queen's quarters, she saw that the queen was upset. On learning about the cause of distress, the seamstress offered to visit England, get back the diamond studs from the duke and return in time for the ball.

Madame Bonacieux took a letter written by the queen to the duke, and asked her husband to deliver it in London. M. Bonacieux refused to do the job and his wife understood that the man had now sworn loyalty to the cardinal.

Just as M. Bonacieux left to inform the cardinal of his wife's actions, d'Artagnan knocked on the door. Madame Bonacieux disclosed in the young Gascon and he volunteered to undertake the task. The lady knew that she could trust d'Artagnan since he had fallen in love with her. So she handed him the letter.

D'Artagnan went straight to M. de Treville's and asked the captain for a leave so that he could complete a mission for Her Majesty. M. de Treville advised him to take the three musketeers along with him so that if there were obstacles on the way at least one of them would be able to complete the mission. D'Artagnan then gathered his friends and they left Paris together.

With great difficulty and many obstacles, d'Artagnan arrived in London. Porthos was detained at a pub on account of a duel, Aramis was shot in the arm and had to rest, while Athos was caught in another surprise attack further ahead.

When d'Artagnan met the duke he handed over the queen's letter to him. After reading the letter, the duke brought out the box of studs. Before handing them over, he opened the box and gave a loud exclamation.

'All is lost!' cried the duke, turning as pale as a corpse. 'Two of the studs are missing; there are only ten here.'

Then he remembered, 'The only time that I had worn these was at a ball, eight days ago. The Countess de Winter, who is one of the cardinal's agents and was present at the ball. She must have stolen them.'

The duke called his goldsmith and ordered him to create exact look-alike of the diamond studs within two days. When the studs had been put back, the duke arranged for d'Artagnan's safe passage back home and the young man arrived in Paris the night before the ball.

The night of the ball was grand and the guests started to arrive by six in the evening. When the queen entered, the king was upset to see that the queen was not wearing the diamond studs. He walked up to her and ordered her to put on the studs immediately.

When the queen left, the cardinal handed over the two stolen diamond studs to the king and asked him to count the number of studs that

the queen has on her. However, to the cardinal's surprise the queen returned wearing all twelve studs. To cover up his folly, the cardinal explained that he had wished to gift the queen the two diamond studs, but considered it rude to do so himself. Therefore, he had devised this plan.

Later, the queen called d'Artagnan and gave him a ring as a token of her gratitude for bringing the studs back. When d'Artagnan returned to his apartment, Planchet handed him a letter. The letter was from Madame Bonacieux, inviting him to meet her in the evening, around ten o'clock.

At the appointed spot, d'Artagnan waited for Madame Bonacieux for an hour. Growing anxious, he looked around and found cracks in the road caused by carriage marks and a lady's glove thrown aside. Worried, d'Artagnan asked a man in a nearby cottage to tell what had occurred there. The man told the Gascon that some men in a carriage had carried off the woman waiting there. From the descriptions given by the man d'Artagnan concluded that it was M. Bonacieux and the man with the scar, known as Comte of Rochefort, who had kidnapped his lady love. d'Artagnan returned, worried but clueless.

One day, d'Artagnan spotted Milady getting into a carriage and heard her order the coachman to drive to St Germain. The young Gascon with his servant followed her, confident that she could lead him to Madame Bonacieux. He found her arguing with a man on horseback and offered to intercede. Milady told d'Artagnan that the man was her brother. However, the two men got into an argument and agreed to a fight behind the Luxembourg Palace.

D'Artagnan arrived, along with the three musketeers, behind the Luxembourg Palace at the decided hour. The Gascon fought a duel with the man, Lord de Winter, while the three musketeers took care of de Winter's friends. The four inseparables defeated their opponents, but d'Artagnan spared the life of Lord de Winter, while declaring that he loved the man's sister. Lord de Winter was grateful and promised to arrange a meeting between the Gascon and his sister, Milady Clarik.

When d'Artagnan met her at her apartment, Milady played the part of a good hostess. So, the young man began paying her a visit every day. Meanwhile, Milady's maid, Kitty, had fallen in love with the young Gascon. Kitty told d'Artagnan that Milady was in love with another man, the Comte de Wardes. One day, she allowed d'Artagnan to overhear a conversation in which Milday told that she met the young Gascon happily because the cardinal wanted him to be dealt with carefully.

The following day, d'Artagnan and his friends were sent on different warfronts to fight France's battle against England. D'Artagnan was ambushed twice, but he escaped and caught one of his attackers. The assassin disclosed that it was Milady who had planned the murderous attacks

on the Gascon. From his attacker, d'Artagnan also learnt that the queen had saved Madame Bonacieux and that she was now safe.

One evening, when d'Artagnan was away on duty, the three Musketeers ran into the cardinal, who made them wait at an inn while he tended to some business. Athos overheard the cardinal talking to Milday. The cardinal told the lady to go to England and ask the Duke of Buckingham to withdraw his troops from France. He added that if the duke refused to surrender, Milady should murder the duke. The lady was eager to do the cardinal the favour, but in turn asked the cardinal to kill d'Artagnan and Madame Bonacieux. The cardinal agreed.

Athos, Porthos and Aramis returned to the warfront and, along with d'Artagnan, kept the English soldiers at bay. Athos also informed the young Gascon all that he had learnt. When they returned to their camp, the three Musketeers were greeted with joy and d'Artagnan was promoted to be a musketeer. All four were delighted.

However, d'Artagnan soon returned to the subject of the murder and insisted that since the queen liked the duke, measures must be taken to prevent his murder. So Aramis sent a letter to his lady love, the queen's seamstress, and told her that the queen must send a warning letter to the duke.

The queen thanked Aramis and his friends and confirmed that she had sent a warning. Another warning letter was sent to Lord de Winter.

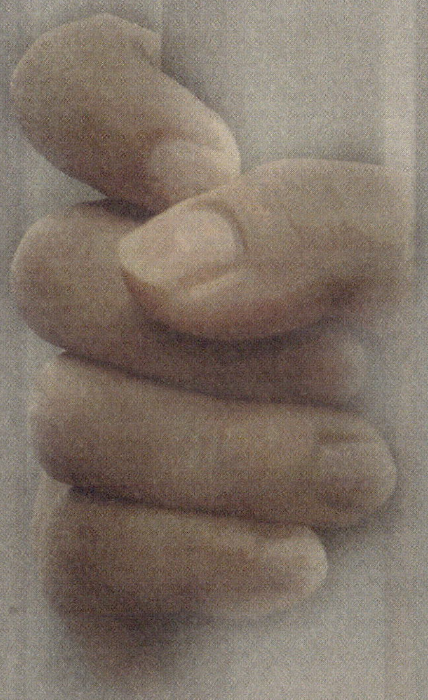

When he was made aware of Milady's dubious plans, de Winter jailed her in England and appointed a trusted officer, Felton, to keep vigil on Milady. However, Milady succeeded in capturing Felton and the officer fell in love with her. One night, Felton set Milady free and told her that he would kill the duke for her. Felton entered the duke's chambers, using Lord de Winter's name, and stabbed him. However, he ran into de Winter on the stairs, who seeing Felton's blood-covered hands understood everything.

Unaware of the duke's death, the four musketeers decided to meet Madame Bonacieux who, they had found out, was in a convent at Bethune. Thus, taking leave from M. de Treville the four musketeers embarked on a journey to Bethune.

Meanwhile, Milady reached the convent at Bethune and learnt that the woman there was the one whom d'Artagnan was in love with. Milady added a drop of poison to a glass of wine and offered this to Madame Bonacieux.

Just then, she heard the sound of hoofs and spotted d'Artagnan and his friends outside the convent. Milady quickly escaped through the back door. When d'Artagnan arrived, Madame Bonacieux described her companion, Milady, to him. Then she died in the young Gascon's arms.

The next day, d'Artagnan discovered Milady's hiding place and along with his friends and Lord de Winter, who had joined them, caught her. Everyone agreed that she deserved a death penalty and so she was executed with one stroke of the sword.

The news of the duke's death had spread far and wide and with it the English forces fell weak. They pulled back and Paris stood victorious in the war.

One day, Comte de Rochefort arrested d'Artagnan for favouring the Duke of Buckingham. At the cardinal's palace, d'Artagnan spoke aloud about Milady's evil actions and showed the cardinal a letter he had which Athos had taken away from Milady. The letter had been written by the cardinal himself and revealed his role in the duke's murder.

The cardinal tore the note and issued d'Artagnan a letter of promotion to the post of lieutenant.

Lieutenant d'Artagnan fought three duels with Comte de Rochefort and won them all. Eventually, the two forgot their past differences and became friends.

D'Artagnan proved to be one of the bravest and the noblest lieutenant of his period. Though he fought many wars and battles, the memories of the time spent with his friends always remained with him.

Other Titles *in the* Series

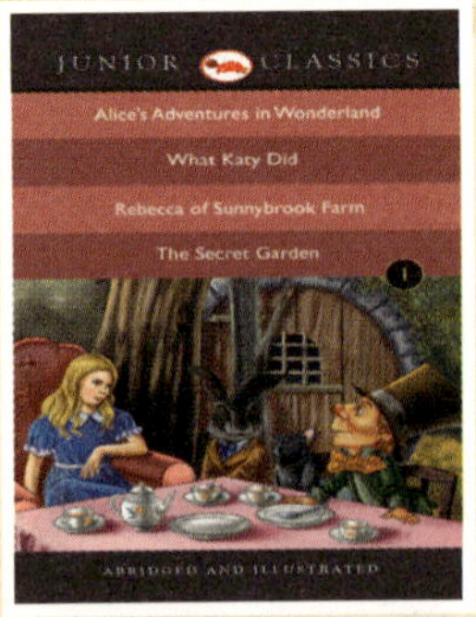

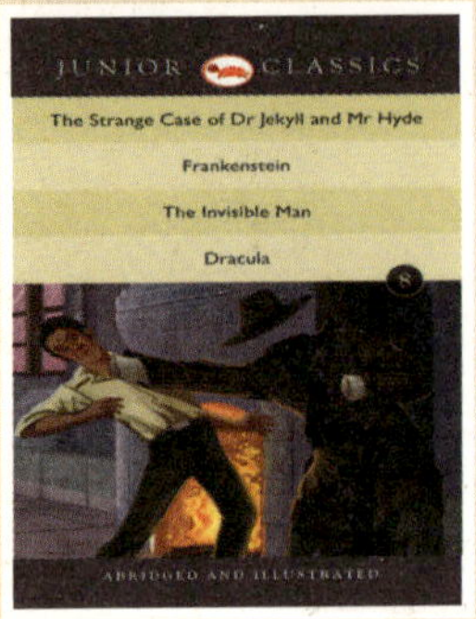